10|31

"The latest installment in Annette Blair's Vintage Magic Mysteries brings back all the things I love about this series: great characters, co~~~~~~ fashion, intriguing mystery, and just a touch of r~~~~~~~~~~~~~~~~~~~ for any fan of cozy mysteries." ~~~~~~~~~~~~~~~~~~~~~~~~~~~~~ _tion_

"Five stars! This s~~~~~~~~~~~~~~~~~~~~~~~~~ ome romance in their ~~~~~~~~~~~~~~~~~~~~~~~~ nor-mal . . . Wheneve~~~~~~~~~~~~~~~~~~~~~~ real world fades away, and I am g~~~~~~~~~~~~~~~~~ nter-tained." —_Huntress Reviews_

"Blair never disappoints. Her books are fun and light-hearted, even though the subject matter can sometimes be dark—the writing is superb, colorful, and bright, making you want more with each page you turn."

—_Fang-tastic Books_

"A well-drawn-out mystery featuring likable characters, and offers a healthy dose of humor and even some vintage fashion tips . . . Annette Blair is a very skilled author, and the story, while complex, comes together nicely at the end."

—_MyShelf.com_

Death by Diamonds

"Annette Blair has the magic touch when it comes to enter-taining joie de vivre paranormal amateur-sleuth whodun-its. The mystery is cleverly constructed."

—_The Best Reviews_

continued . . .

"A wonderful investigative tale that will have armchair readers spellbound . . . With whimsy, humor, and Dante to round out the magic, fans will enjoy this entertaining paranormal amateur sleuth."
—*The Best Reviews*

"A joy to read."
—*Gumshoe Review*

A Veiled Deception

"Whimsical, witty, and wonderful . . . Sure to enchant readers everywhere."
—Madelyn Alt, national bestselling
author of *Home for a Spell*

"A wonderful book . . . A literary whisper adds to the charm."
—*RT Book Reviews*

"Not only a good start to a new series but a great example of the supernatural mystery genre."
—*Curled Up with a Good Book*

"Annette Blair brings her characters to vivid life . . . Fun, witty, and highly recommended."
—*Huntress Reviews*

"A smart, funny start to a new series . . . Cleverly plotted."
—*The Mystery Reader*

"Phenomenal. Ms. Blair beautifully captures New England's ambiance and mystique as she weaves a well-crafted mystery into the threads of Maddie Cutler's life."
—*Fresh Fiction*

"A funny, engaging read. Annette Blair puts together a mystery with humor, suspense, and quite the engaging plot . . . The dialogue is witty, there's humor throughout the story, along with friendship and family, sexual tension without the story revolving around the sex, and the plot just zings along."
—*ParaNormal Romance*

TULLE DEATH
Do Us Part

ANNETTE BLAIR

BERKLEY PRIME CRIME, NEW YORK

THE BERKLEY PUBLISHING GROUP
Published by the Penguin Group
Penguin Group (USA) Inc.
375 Hudson Street, New York, New York 10014, USA

USA | Canada | UK | Ireland | Australia | New Zealand | India | South Africa | China

Penguin Books Ltd., Registered Offices: 80 Strand, London WC2R 0RL, England
For more information about the Penguin Group, visit penguin.com.

TULLE DEATH DO US PART

A Berkley Prime Crime Book / published by arrangement with the author

Berkley Prime Crime Books are published by The Berkley Publishing Group.
BERKLEY® PRIME CRIME and the PRIME CRIME
logo are trademarks of Penguin Group (USA) Inc.

For information, address: The Berkley Publishing Group,
a division of Penguin Group (USA) Inc.,
375 Hudson Street, New York, New York 10014.

ISBN: 978-0-425-25193-5

PUBLISHING HISTORY
Berkley Prime Crime mass-market edition / July 2013

PRINTED IN THE UNITED STATES OF AMERICA

10 9 8 7 6 5 4 3 2 1

Cover illustration by Ben Perini.
Cover design by Rita Frangie.
Interior text design by Laura K. Corless.

This is a work of fiction. Names, characters, places, and incidents either are the product
of the author's imagination or are used fictitiously, and any resemblance to actual persons,
living or dead, business establishments, events, or locales is entirely coincidental.
The publisher does not have any control over and does not assume any responsibility for
author or third-party websites or their content.

ALWAYS LEARNING   **PEARSON**

With love to:
Teresa Christina Areia and Scott Christopher Blair,
now known as Mr. and Mrs. Scott Blair,
on the happy (read delirious) occasion of your wedding.
Welcome my new daughter. Welcome my new grandson.
Expanding the family is a dream come true.
And so are you.

Author's Note

Historic Mystic, Connecticut, is a treat, as is the Mystic River, both well worth a visit. Mystick Falls, to the north, however, is a figment of my imagination, as are the locations of my characters' homes and of the town's governing body. I have too much respect for the real governing body to portray them any other way.

One

Last night, I bedazzled a hard hat. Crystals, and sequins, and bling. Oh my.

What else to wear to a roof-raising with black tuxedo-cut Hilfiger overalls, a tux shirt, and a pair of black velvet Belgian loafers? I mean, my Vintage Magic dress shop is now a construction zone. I have to be practical and fashion conscious.

Of course, the unseasonably mild February weather, even for so short a jaunt outdoors, called for a mohair scarf from the English Lake District, and kid gloves, both in maize and neutral.

According to family legend, I've been a fashionista since they cut the cord, anointed me in sweet baby oil, and wrapped me in pink to match the bow in my hair. Then I grew up and became . . . well . . . a fashionista, the designing kind. Take that any way you like. I do.

I sell designer vintage classics, preferably haute couture, and personally design fashion-forward one-of-a-kind originals. Designing also applies to the way I deal with the charming legacy bequeathed to me by my late mother, a discovery with *witch* I try daily to make a certain peace. That gift is not limited to "listening" to whatever vintage fashions "speak to me" and using those visions to help solve crimes, often as antique as my sources.

My name is Madeira Cutler, but I prefer Mad or Maddie. Only my dad, Harry Cutler, lit-quoting University of Connecticut professor, uses my full name, whether I want him to or not.

I expected Dad to join me any minute on the Bank Street sidewalk, across from my corner shop. Meanwhile, on Main Street, crowded with tourists and locals, I noticed an odd duck whose Armani suit might as well have been made of flashing neon. Though I couldn't get a good look at it, it was still obvious that he so did not fit in.

Figuring he had a right to be there, I leaned against Mystic Pizza's dove-gray clapboards sipping hot coffee while my building took on the brightening glow of dawn's early light.

Eve Meyers, my pixie-cut strawberry-blonde BFF, a steampunk goth computer genius, snapped pictures of the roof-raising with a tech-forward camera that could do everything but pipe a seam.

Wearing Blahnik booties and a black corseted jodhpur jumpsuit of my design, Eve had an eye for two things: photography and men in hard hats. Unfortunately, the crew kept their eyes on her, too. She'd nearly been banned from the site twice now. The workers had the injuries to prove it.

My former morgue-cum-funeral-chapel carriage house, a study in lavender and sage, would have looked positively poetic, except for the swarm of construction workers crawling over it like ants at a cupcake picnic.

Judging from the salty funk in the air, low tide and dawn had arrived at the same time this morning.

"Wish I could live in one of your new apartments," Eve said.

My third floor would accommodate three. I raised a brow, and she shrugged.

Her parents came from the old country. In their perfect world, Eve would leave after a traditional wedding and move into her husband's house. Not gonna happen, given Eve's allergic reaction to convention.

Not that she can't catch a man; she often stands corset-deep in them. She simply likes the challenge of changing them as often as her hair color.

Me, I needed to move on, and not just because Dad had moved in with Fiona, the second love of his life and my second mom after my own mom passed away when I was a kid. It was practically a proposal, and my dad was selling our historic old tavern house to my brother Alex so he and his wife Trish could raise their kids there. No more traveling. Alex had transferred to a specialized FBI field installation in our area and now came home every night.

I refused to move in with either couple, though I'd been invited. Fiona, better known as Aunt Fee, is not my biological aunt. She was my mother's college BFF, her sister witch, and later, a "mom in a storm" for four motherless Cutler kids. Still is—twenty years after my mother's passing. She and my dad fought for most of those years—it was the witch thing—but over time, the fighting took a 360. Fiona, well, she's loved Dad since before he met my mother. Nuff said.

As a result, I was building three third-floor apartments above my shop. I'd live in one and rent the other two for the income.

The gathering crowd gasped, bringing me back to my new digs while Eve's camera snapped a soothing soundtrack. The misplaced executive type, like an ad for five-grand suits, stood so intensely focused on my roof, I had to wonder what he thought he'd see.

Could he be one of Eve's latest? He sure didn't seem the type to dance at the end of one of her man-strings, though she'd brought home worse and scarier.

In a traffic-stopping stunt, my roof was being raised above my building, held aloft by long-armed orange whirligigs, while a prefab third-floor outer wall was slipped beneath it to meet my attic floor.

"Almost there," Eve whispered, as if she might jinx it by speaking too loudly.

Dad and Aunt Fiona joined me, with my little Chakra in her cat carrier for safety's sake. Fiona came up behind me and slipped a black velvet cape over my shoulders. My father hooked it beneath the scarf at my chin.

Aunt Fee beamed. "I told you, Harry, that she'd need it."

"It was your mother's, Mad," my father said, knuckling my cheek. "Fee's been keeping it for you. I agree, it's time for you to have it."

Whoa. I stroked the full-length cape, one surely worn for Wiccan rituals, and I pulled it tight around me. "It's like Mom's hugging me, Daddy."

He pulled me into his arms, and I inhaled the comforting scent of cherry pipe tobacco.

"Stop!" Isaac, the construction boss, shouted, getting our attention in a big way.

"Stop!" an assortment of foremen echoed, one after another.

"Something's in the way," Isaac shouted.

And didn't the exec across the street jump like the boogeyman just said "Boo!" and then stop breathing and moving . . . frozen, like somebody had stabbed him in the back with an ice pick?

Unexpectedly, our gazes locked—mine and Odd Duck's—and, looking stricken, he disappeared into the crowd.

I stopped breathing myself, for two reasons: The man spooked me royally, and my roof-raising had come to a dead halt. "Inches away and they can't make it work?" I snapped, stepping off the curb to cross the street.

Dad caught my arm. "Wait," he said. " 'Fools rush in' and all that. Hear what Issac has to say first. It's dangerous over there."

Lip-biting and silent, I nodded and stepped back onto the curb, while the workers jostled a fragile puzzle consisting of heavy equipment and assorted building parts.

One mistake and they could wipe out my savings account, like, forever.

At the Main and Bank Street corner of my attic, Isaac knelt, looked my way, and raised a wait-a-minute finger.

While my heart beat like an Olympic runner's, I saluted my response. Never let them see you sweat.

Eve kept snapping pics, the reliable cadence of clicks

combined with the lullaby of mom's cape flapping around my legs to have a reassuring effect on me.

Isaac tugged something from the corner rafters, his shout one of success, and with both hands, he held up a package. The crew cheered, as did the watching crowd. Even strangers took pictures, reminding me that, once again, I'd changed the face of Main Street. I'd already turned a derelict eyesore into a vintage beauty that graced brochures. And now I was giving it stature.

Rubberneckers pumped their arms out of car windows, horns blaring. In the distance, boat whistles seemed to respond, adding to the omnipresent *whoosh* of Amtrak's Acela rushing, as if on cue, nonstop through Mystic.

Isaac conferred with his second in command and disappeared from the top of the mark.

When he stepped out my front door, he grinned and cupped a hand around his mouth. "Hey, Mad, bit of buried treasure for ya." He could make himself heard, that man, and people listened. That's why I hired him. That and he worked cheap in winter, because after he walled the third floor, he'd only show up when he had no other work. For that, I got a great price and a great contractor.

I was so focused on the "treasure," I didn't realize I missed the rush of getting a third floor, until half the town of Mystic applauded. I looked at Eve in shock, but she raised her camera with pride, and I knew the moment wasn't lost to me after all.

I hitched up my gloves and closed my cape against the wind. Traffic had picked up speed, but the cars turning onto Bank were stopping, so we could cross to my parking lot.

I thanked Isaac as he shoved the package into my hands

while Chakra swiped her bare claws out the window of her carrier, to claim, or annihilate, the find.

Fiona pulled my butterscotch-striped baby away, but I hadn't named her Chakra for nothing. That cat knew when I was scared, or when I should be, I suppose. And now, because of her reaction, I had that solar plexus tremble that only she could soothe and, evidently, instigate.

I held on to what appeared to be a wrapped box tightly, rather than drop it and risk breaking whatever might be inside. The last unexpected find in this building gave me nightmares still, and I didn't have hope for better with this. So I wouldn't speculate on the contents or reveal them in public.

Eve took pictures of the find at varied angles. She said she had enough memory to take thousands. I presume she meant the camera did, though I'd learned never to sell Eve short.

The treasure looked like a pale, square brick of moiré-a-pois silk appliquéd in a faded peach-and-white single-V chevron motif, applied with tiny, perfect hand stitching, reminiscent of haute couture. Odd to find a Parisian piece used as wrapping paper when newspaper would have done as well.

I pulled back on the suspicious fabric with my gloved hand—glad it was gloved—to reveal a vintage brass box, high quality, topped by a raised and engraved plate, and as I did, the wind whipped the fabric up and swiped it across my face.

Screech! It touched me.

Eve snapped pictures of the box from several angles, then the fabric alone, then the bare box and the engraving.

7

"Mystick by the Sea Country Club, Established 1923," she read, and whistled.

A rush of ice had already run up my neck and, by the time my knees weakened, I was pretty sure that the fabric might once have been a piece of vintage clothing.

"Oh, oh," Aunt Fiona said. "Harry, grab her."

"Not again!" Eve fought me for the box, but I had no control over my hands and held it in something of a death grip, as if rigor mortis had set in.

"I bet that's part of a dress or something!" Eve said. "I hate when this happens!" Her panic tickled me as I slipped from the reality of this plane to another, though, as always, I left my body behind.

"Mad?" she shouted. "Where did you go this time?"

"Eve," my father groused. "She's right here!"

Confession time: My father doesn't know about my psychometric gift or my mother's. Not his thing, Mom used to say.

Right now, it only mattered that everyone swirling away from me. Or, rather, their voices were doing so as I, in my own psychic way, swirled away from them, and found myself . . . where?

A hovel, cold, dark, and dank, barely warmed by the labored breaths of the specters gathered there, their features shadowed like spirits in the belly of a whale. I saw only the whites of their eyes, and my gag reflex was triggered by the overpowering stench of fish, fear, . . . and guilt.

$\mathcal{T}wo$

Over the years I have learned that what is important in a dress is the woman who is wearing it.

—YVES SAINT LAURENT

So whose dress had I stepped into? Whose body? And why did she wear such a tight rubber girdle? Some vintage pieces I didn't appreciate, and here I found myself being strangled by the master, a design horror that rivaled an unsanctioned sweat lodge for dehydration.

Fortunately, these psychic trips I took after touching certain items of vintage clothing never lasted long, which meant I would be out of here soon, so I had to learn as much as I could in very little time.

I caught the tension as I eyed the antsy group and was unable to stand completely still, while having no idea where I stood. Literally. The belly of a boat seemed more likely than a whale. I found limited proof in the fact that I saw no corners in my peripheral vision, though the area could be termed a black pit. As a seafaring vessel, it would have to be good sized, possibly eighty or ninety feet, and though I smelled the sea and heard the waves, I found no need for sea legs.

Midnight had surely come and gone. A quarter moon peeked through a window or a hole in the wall, while a storm rushed nature's fury all around us, the wind howling in the distance without mercy. In other circumstances, the combo might seem romantic, but the copper scent of blood mixed with sweat and brine told a different story.

I'd surely and inadvertently been kissed by a piece of vintage clothing, a secret my building had been keeping since who knew when.

Well, possibly since this moment in which I now found myself, I suppose.

My gift of viewing the past in snippets came more frequent of late, like all aspects of my mother's legacy. These days, rhymes like spells filled my head without warning, especially at moments of high emotion. Not that I knew what to do with them, and I might not be ready to learn. Yet.

Understand that "gift" and "curse" are two sides of the same cold-steel blade, especially at times like this, but Aunt Fiona had convinced me that I had a universal mandate to make the best of each vision. I'd learned that someone or something attached to them depended on me. My job was to find out who, what, or why.

A man in a tattered tux, who might have worn an aftershave called Low Tide and recently fought a saber-toothed shark, filled the center of my vision, his body language giving off edgy vibes. As my eyes adjusted to the darkness, I saw a near circle of followers who seemed to be waiting for their pacing leader's next words.

Why? Because he could be counted upon to get them

out of trouble? Or because he'd been the one to get them into it? Why trouble? Well, the location itself shouted it. This was no shrieking slumber party I'd happened upon.

"Stop assuming the worst," the agitated leader snapped. "She was the best swimmer at Vassar."

The timbre of his voice, as if by shouting his voice alone could ensure the girl's health, had startled us all, especially me, deep in my solar plexus. Instincts kicked in, like I knew him but didn't like him much. The sound of his voice left a bad taste in my mouth, so I found myself referring to him in my mind as Grody.

I sensed that, before my arrival, the group had been contemplating the matter that had instigated Grody's telling statement.

We must be near the sea, I silently reasoned, if someone's swimming ability matters in quite possibly a life-or-death way.

"I'm certain she made it," he muttered, again his voice willing it to be true, adding fear and desperation to his ticket.

Across the circle, a girl whose outline revealed the pouf skirt of a crinolined gown, raised her nose in a perfect show of snobbery. "The second best swimmer!" she snapped, heavy on the snit. Her voice, with its vainglorious tone, also seemed eerily familiar.

I might actually have known the two of them—in the present, I mean. Wow, what were the odds? I shrugged inwardly. In a town this size, I guessed pretty good.

"I"—she pointed to herself—"am the one who captained the Vassar swim team," Vainglory added. "Not Robin."

"Yeah, and you were prom queen, too. We know," said

Grody, still stirring in me a shivery ambivalence, bordering on dislike. Good news/bad news: I thought we'd tangled at some point, but I couldn't place him.

And the "we" could be debated. "We" as in he and Madeira Cutler? Or "we" as in Grody and the person I now occupied?

With vagaries and misdeeds in mind, I wished uselessly for a full moon so I could see all their faces, certain, given their furtive energy—not forgetting the swimmer they wanted to believe had reached shore—that they did not want the lights on.

Why? So as not to be found trespassing? Or not to be caught for their misdeed?

"What about G.I. Joe?" Grody asked. "Does he know his girl left the fiftieth with . . . you know?"

"No," Vainglory said. "Uniforms draw attention. He couldn't get away from the girls at the bar—especially Wynona—and had his back to us when Prince Charmy lured Robin from the country club."

"He'll be looking for her now, then, won't he?"

Vainglory gave one inelegant snort. "He shipped out at midnight, none the wiser. Done deed."

"I forgot," Grody said. "On his way to Nam, poor devil, though they say it's nearly over." And the heartless man sounded almost sorry for a soldier who'd lost his last night with his girl, and maybe a future with her, too—if she couldn't swim, however far, in storm-tossed waters.

Nam? Toward the end. If that was true, I had quite possibly stepped into the early seventies.

"Some scavenger hunt," said a young man with a slight Southern baritone. "Bor-ing." His careless attitude curled around me like a get-it-off-me reptile. Icy, slimy, icky. "Did we get anything good at least?" Snake asked.

He thought some tangible good could come from this? I shivered. One of them might be drowning, and he was whining to know what they had netted.

"Why are we here?" another girl asked. "Shouldn't we have scattered?"

"We're here," Grody said, "to get our stories straight."

"Better if they're all different," Vainglory said. "We'll each stash our own spoils, after all."

"Temporarily," Grody added. "Don't go getting attached. The goods have to be returned to their owners as soon as we know who wins."

Not Robin, I thought. It sounded like she might have come out the loser in all this.

Vainglory tittered. "Hide your trinkets well, or this could be embarrassing in the morning."

Embarrassing? Someone could quite possibly be dead by morning, and they were going to wait it out? "Shouldn't we call the police?" the person I occupied asked, while the same question sat at the tip of my silent tongue. Made me hope my thoughts influenced hers.

Vainglory tittered again.

Call me a fake Ferragamo, but I could almost name the vain one, given her superior tone and familiar disdain.

Grody, the leader? He fit a memory as substantial as fiberfill. Vainglory, on the other hand, cut a bloodier swath, like machine stitching through a thumbnail. But she must have left Mystick Falls by now, because I had the good fortune to have blocked our shared past, er, future.

For some reason I was more Madeira in this vision than the person I was wearing, not a strong character at all.

Vainglory chuckled, as if mocking the thought, and I knew that nothing good could come of her amusement. To prove me right, I saw her in shadow as she tugged and slithered from one of her bell-shaped petticoats. She waved it like a victory flag and chuckled while my heart sped to the subsequent sickening sound of fabric tearing.

"Your mother's going to kill you," said the woman I occupied, her kind voice jarringly out of place in this viper's den. "Isn't that gown worth a fortune? She keeps it encased in glass. It's her most prized possession." My body for the evening, totally unknown to me, caught her breath and I caught her sorrow. "Did your mother give you permission to wear that? Or did you steal it?"

"I borrowed it," Vainglory said with a purring lilt of self-satisfaction, and I knew instinctively that her amusement showed as a grin laced with evil. "Don't sweat it, and don't be a fink, Bambi-Jo. I'm not tearing the gown after all, just the matching petticoat."

"The matching petticoat?" Bambi-Jo asked.

"Of course. It's huge. There'll be lots of pieces when I'm done with it. We'll each have enough to wrap and hide our scavenged items in. At least it will have gone for a good cause." She dropped it to the floor. "There, everyone. Tear it into as many pieces as you need."

Vainglory proceeded to wrap her first fabric piece around a trinket. "After we send everything we borrowed to the country club—let them return our spoils to their members—I plan to send the petticoat back to my darling mother piece by piece, month by entertaining month."

Bambi-Jo squeaked beneath her breath, and I wondered how this nice, if mousy, girl got mixed up with this set.

"Here, Bambi, you take and hide this. I think it's the biggest item we scavenged tonight, except for Robin herself, of course."

Robin, the Vassar swimmer who could be drowning. Who might now be safe, or not.

"How long have we been here?" I thought and Bambi asked. Coincidence?

Vainglory huffed. "You know very well that we only left the country club's Golden Jubilee dinner dance a few hours ago." She shoved a prewrapped box into my hands—well, Bambi-Jo's hands—as if my question had ticked her off. It was the same box that had brought me here. Oh oh. So as not to rush off, psychically speaking, I handed it to the unnamed person next to me. Let's call him Brut, because that's what he so overwhelmingly smelled like. I wanted to stick around a little longer. I had too many questions to leave now. Who were all these players, and who was the smarm who had lured Robin to sea?

And what were the results of Robin's unexpected swim?

"I hid a scavenger-hunt list in that box," said Brut, "for posterity. Don't get blood on it." Then he shoved it back into my hands, cover and all, while his voice grew distant and my vision wavered.

Three

Ready or not, and bound by frustration, I parted company
with the felons in the belly of the whale, the distance
between us widening by the minute. Literally. Physically.
In miles and in time.

My ears rang as my shop came into focus, and I saw my
father standing over me.

I adjusted my position on the fainting couch while Dad
held the lecture stance, serious, determined, professorial
words pouring forth, as if . . . as if he'd been trying to talk
me into doing my homework, or taking a part in one of his
dreaded impromptu Shakespearean plays.

"So," he said, sounding relieved to have finished.
"That's why you'll make the perfect judge."

"Judge?" I asked. "Fiona's the judge, not me." I sat up,
almost glad I'd returned from the back of beyond, from possibly as close as the Mystic docks yet as far as decades ago.

I must have been looking at my dad like he spoke in tongues. I knew Aunt Fiona understood my confusion, but only when I gave her a slight wave did she realize that I was truly back. All of me. My mind and everything.

She knew I'd checked out for a time, though my dad hadn't figured it out. Probably thought I was resting my eyes, or Fee told him I was.

I heard the hammers and heavy equipment above us and, despite my trip to the past, I was glad for the progression of my third floor. Well, my fourth floor, if you counted the old county morgue some people called my basement, a floor I'd not yet seen. Horror for another day, and all that.

I shuddered and put the morgue from my mind. "Aunt Fiona? What does Dad think I'm judging? Which, by the way, I'm not . . . judging, that is."

My father slapped his hands on his hips. "Haven't you been listening? By Zeus, your attention span needs a recharge. I can't believe you've got an MBA."

As far as my father was concerned, my degree in fashion design didn't count for much. No biggie. It counted big time in the glamazon world of designer vintage.

Chakra settled against my solar plexus to soothe me while she kept raising her paws toward the fabric-covered treasure box on the floor. Finally, she pounced on it and rolled with the fabric. "Dad, can you get that away from her?"

He did and set it on the counter. "Aren't you going to open the box?" he asked.

Given my previous experience with opening things and finding, well, people parts, I wanted to open Pandora's newest surprise like I wanted a root canal.

A better bet would be to have Detective Lytton Werner

by my side with a Dos Equis in each of our hands. I was suddenly glad it had been wrapped. That meant the box itself could be dusted for prints. And I'd handled it with gloves—in this world, at least. Although the spoiled brats of the past should have been wearing gloves, I didn't remember having noticed any.

Aunt Fiona lowered herself to the foot of the fainting couch and patted my hand. "It's about judging vintage formals for the country club's Very Vintage Valentine fun- and fund-raiser, dear. It's a 'remember the old days' dinner with music for dancing, and a bit of a show while we eat, a *This Is Your Life* segment—"

My father ran a hand over his face.

Fee tried to look more enthusiastic. "You probably don't remember the programs, dear, but they'd put the contestant in a comfy chair with a cup of tea and some refreshments, make them sit back, and a voice from the past would come from behind a curtain. Like, 'Remember me? I took you on your first pony ride.'"

My father huffed. "And the contestant goes, 'Nanny Carousel?' Ta-da, here comes old Nanny Carousel, who the contestant hasn't seen in eleventy-seven years, and they have a teary reunion, and so on. It's all voices and people from the past ad nauseam."

"Wow," Fiona said. "Harry, you sure know how to neutralize the anticipation."

My father looked contrite. "It *is* more exciting than that," he admitted to me. "I just wanted it said fast, so we could get down to business with a yes from you, Mad." His look pleaded with me. "What do you say?"

Fee sighed in exasperation. "Yes, that's where you come

in." She gave me a "there, there" pat because she understood my qualms because of my visions. "The event will benefit the foundation that your sister Brandy works for," she said. The children will get the ticket proceeds minus expenses."

"The Nurture Kids Foundation." I remembered. "A good cause, feeding hungry children." It would be harder to say no now, but not impossible. I'd make a personal donation if my refusal jinxed Brandy's cause.

"Correct." Aunt Fee winked "That's the exact foundation."

"I told you we're chairing the event," my dad snapped, frustrated at repeating himself, except that I hadn't *been here* in the true sense. "I told you that new members of the country club have to do their share." He was also probably frustrated with Fee for volunteering them. "Not my idea!" he added, proving it.

Do I know my dad or what?

I chuckled because I had been right, while Aunt Fiona gave him a saucy grin.

He eyed her with false malevolence, though I recognized that twinkle in his eyes. The look predicted a pithy quote. "'A fine horse or a beautiful woman,'" he said. "'I cannot look at them unmoved, even now when seventy winters have chilled my blood.'" Dad crossed his arms as if to rest his case. "Not that I'm as old as Sir Arthur Conan Doyle when he said it."

Aunt Fee laughed, stood, and cupped my dad's cheeks. "I have a quote, too." She cleared her throat, not letting go of his face. "'She would have despised the modern idea of women being equal to men. Equal, indeed! She knew they

19

were superior.' " Aunt Fee kissed my dad's cheek. "So said Elizabeth Gaskell, and so say I."

For Aunt Fee, I applauded. Lord of the Bling, she had him. She had my father in the palm of her hand. By giving as good as she got, she'd been offered his surrendered heart on a gold platter. Quoting him back—a trick my mother had never tried.

That's what Dad had needed to wake up and smell the latte: Aunt Fee standing alone, separate in his mind, once and for all, from Mom.

I stood, hugged her, and elbowed my frowning dad, as if he and I shared a joke. I loved his stubborn sense of denial. He really did it for Fiona. He filled her heart to overflowing. And in turn, she did the same for him.

For them, I should judge whatever they wanted me to. For myself, well, I should shout "No!" like any normal daughter. "Why exactly do you want me to judge?" I asked, in case I caved, which I hoped I wouldn't.

Aunt Fee stepped away from Dad, her cheeks rosy as she smoothed her Westwood pencil skirt. "More entrants than we can manage want to participate in the country club's *This Is Your Life* segment," she said. "There can only be five participants. So we made you the golden ticket, well . . . a 'chosen by Madeira Cutler' piece of vintage clothing is the ticket. In order to win, the entrant must wear a piece that was worn to the club's original Golden Jubilee, which we're modeling our event after. The Golden Jubilee celebrated the club's fiftieth anniversary."

Aunt Fiona touched my arm. "We thought those with the best vintage outfits would have had the most interesting lives."

My father cleared his throat. "You must admit, Madeira, it's better than putting names in a hat, and the winners will wear their original vintage outfits during the segment."

"How are you going to discover their life stories to do the segment?" I asked, thinking of my psychometric trip back in time to another Golden Jubilee night—well, the aftermath, anyway—the one Dad and Fee now wanted to replicate with their Very Vintage Valentine fund-raiser.

On the other hand, what they learned about the event's history could very well help me figure out what was already starting to feel like another mandate from the universe, a sleuthing expedition.

"Fee and I are the show hosts and therefore the researchers," Dad stressed, teeth grinding as he spoke. "So the entrants are giving us significant dates and family histories, honors and awards, spouses and so forth, the important life points of reference."

"I think you should ask them to describe the original Golden Jubilee as they remember it, if the winners were actually there," I suggested. "I wish I could interview them with you. But I can't see it happening with my schedule. Take really good, detailed notes while doing your research. 'Kay?"

Aunt Fee gave me a double take and hid a knowing grin, though she failed to dim her interest. She knew I'd just been to the past. She knew that I knew . . . something.

"Mad, they'll have to give you their winning outfits to refurbish and alter. So you'll spend time with them, do the fittings, ask some questions. Oh, and you can charge your regular prices, while introducing some very well-to-do people to your shop."

We both smiled.

"We made a deal," she continued, "that you get to display their outfits after the event. You can make the outfits part of your Valentine's Day display for the church's candlelight city tour the weekend after the holiday. It was such a smart marketing idea for you to enter your historic building as a stop on the tour."

That would save me a great deal of fuss at a busy time, this judging thing making it worse. The Valentine house tour was only a few days after this country club event. I gave her a nod of approval. "Thanks."

"No one will see the outfits twice, because the country-club set aren't the ones who take the tours," she said. "They'll be at home showing off their houses."

"Well played, Aunt Fiona." And I meant it in several ways.

She preened. "But their relatives will surely come to your shop to see their family history on display," she continued. "Which can net you some great new customers."

"I can trump that," my father said. "This event is bigger than you think. Everyone who was ever a member of the country club has been invited from wherever they live in the world right now."

"Why?" I asked. "Is this an anniversary year?"

"No, but in the spring, the country club's breaking ground for a new building, so they're creating warm feelings for their contribution to the community, family style. In case anybody wants to 'invest.' Friend-raising, you could call it."

"I should have known it would come down to money," I grumbled.

Aunt Fee stepped, without thought, into my dad's arms, and he, without thought, closed his arms around her. "Doesn't it always?" she asked.

"I suppose." I crossed the back of the shop and took a bottle of green tea from my mini fridge, offered it around— no takers—and sipped it myself. "So the five people participating in the *This Is Your Life* portion of the evening dress in vintage outfits from the Golden Jubilee, but what does everyone else wear? Vintage clothes from any era?"

"They can wear what they wore to the fiftieth, if they want, or whatever best represents their own history." My dad chuckled. "I can just imagine the preponderance of academic robes," he said.

Aunt Fee nodded in surprise. "That's true. I plan to suggest military uniforms, as well, so I can thank people for their service to our country."

"Make thanking them part of the event," I said. "They and their families will appreciate it."

While my father and Aunt Fee congratulated each other on my brilliance, I realized that attendees would feel safe playing dress-up, because who knew that clothes had tales to tell? "I hope I'll have plenty of time to examine the outfits submitted for the *This Is Your Life* segment?"

"Of course. Eve and I intend to help you," Fiona said. "You know, handle what you tell us to." She gave me that "between us" look, because she knew there would be certain clothing items I might not want to touch.

"Come on, Mad, say yes," she urged. "We're also going to have a contest on the night of the event, and there'll be prizes for the best vintage outfits. Most outrageous, most original, most famous designer, greatest vintage find, best one of a kind." Aunt Fee bit her lip. "Will you be on the panel to judge those, too? You'll love the event! Think of the outfits you'll get to see and you get to wear your favorite yourself."

My father squeezed her waist, like maybe she shouldn't have told me about the second round of judging quite yet. Then he pulled me against his other side. "Nobody can judge vintage clothes like you can, dumplin'."

"Oh, bring out the big guns. When I'm Daddy's dumplin', I'm ruffled and starched."

"Is that a yes?" he asked.

"No, but you can keep trying."

"As we said, you only have to choose five *This Is Your Life*rs," Aunt Fiona said. "That's all we'll have time to get into the segment."

"You have some pretty good arguments, but I have a better one: I can only choose one. I'll alienate half my local clientele. They're my bread and butter."

Aunt Fiona's grin grew. "You won't be choosing people, dear. You'll be choosing anonymously owned outfits."

I couldn't stop my shoulders from sagging. It had been a long day, and I was worried about a girl named Robin. I didn't need this pressure, too.

From her caramel lizard-skin box bag by Nettie Rosenstein, Aunt Fiona took a stack of assorted photos—square, oblong, jagged- and straight-edged, dated and not, with some streaked old Polaroids we had to squint at to see.

Fee didn't know it, but I probably would have caved sooner if I'd noticed her carrying the bag I gave her for her birthday. In the fifties, that Nettie Rosenstein bag was a pricey sought-after piece of vintage magic.

I perused the photos, some color, some black-and-white, with an unbiased eye and great interest. Several group candids and posed shots, then pictures of attendees dancing in an awesome assortment of gorgeous vintage formals, the kind you wore crinolines beneath. My heart picked up speed, until the sight of one, where just the hint of a chevron pattern made me sit hard on my mom's old wing-back chair behind me.

I believed in Aunt Fee's sense that my psychometric gift was a mandate from the universe, but did I have to get hit upside the head with it?

Four

I examined the next photo, one that would literally change the course of my life. Sleuthing always did, and all I needed to see, in its full backlit glory, was a color shot of a gown with a gather of peach and white with that rare chevron striped design appliquéd to it, over an embroidered crepe silk peach gown.

I looked down at the box on the floor beside me and knew—I just knew—that the paler version of chevron stripes on silk moiré-a-pois belonged to that very special petticoat, the one designed—and hand-stitched in Paris, I believed—to be worn beneath that very special haute couture gown.

So . . . at least one petticoat piece had never been mailed back to Vainglory's mother.

The existence of the box, in a place that had been an abandoned building at the time, might also indicate that none of the "borrowed" treasures had ever been returned.

How many other trinkets, as Vainglory had called them, and Golden Jubilee outfits were still out there, and what kind of stories did they have to tell?

If I said yes to my father and Aunt Fiona, would I learn more guilty secrets from that Golden Jubilee scavenger hunt, or had my first trip to the past been an isolated vision?

If that gown with the chevron stripes came to me—to judge now, or at the ball later—I might be able to find out.

I hadn't wanted to be a judge because I didn't want my customers to feel I had favorites. I didn't want to risk alienating any of them. Also, I'd disliked my vision; the people in it; their cavalier, entitled attitudes; the lack of respect for the rights of others.

Essentially, I did not want to sleuth the forty-year-old country club event. I'd bet the club had seen more than their fair share of bored-rich-kid scavenger hunts over the years. I just wondered how many had ended in the loss of a life.

Yet, more than I disliked the scenario, I wanted to know if a Vassar swimmer named Robin had survived the sea on one particular stormy night. And I definitely wanted to know what, or who, caused her to jump into the briny deep in the first place.

So, I thought, how could I do worse? For a donation to the Nurture Kids Foundation, I might also find the unknown slimeball who'd led Robin to plunge into the ocean, and bring him to justice.

I sighed. "Dad, Fiona, I will judge the vintage formal wear contest for you. I won't like it, but I'll do it, if"—I raised a finger—"you let me see the research on your *This Is Your Life* candidates. Give me that option, and I'll even be on the panel to judge the rest of the outfits on the night of the event. That's my only request."

"Done," Aunt Fiona said while she and my dad high-fived each other.

"How romantic," I remarked with snark.

Oh, the look they gave each other; it warmed a daughter's heart.

I think for a minute they forgot I was there, but I had plenty to occupy my mind.

It seemed too much of a coincidence, I thought, all of this happening at once. But we live in a wily universe, we do; a real schemer. All kinds of things happening that we don't understand or believe. Spirits of loved ones walking about, nudging us to go on, holding us when we cry. Past and present colliding and, more often than not, going so far as to knock us about. Then the spirits help us get our heads on straight again.

So much we don't know.

Maybe the love of vintage clothes—their histories in particular—started me on this path when, at the age of ten, I refused to give my dead mother's clothes to a secondhand shop like my dad wanted. Maybe with that I set my mom's legacy free. Who knows?

Maybe my dad and Aunt Fiona found each other because she offered to store my mom's clothes, which were the items with which I would begin my vintage shop. Maybe Aunt Fee had started the hand of fate manipulating psychic ripples in the universal waters of life. Like a rock tossed into a lake, the circles had grown bigger and reached me today in the form of a box, whose wrapper I touched and to whose past I journeyed, where I'd seen the box's wrapper as a whole, a petticoat, and its match, the gown, as it had once been. A beauty that should not have been desecrated. A haute couture gown—priceless—in the hands of a careless brat.

Surely my gifts grew stronger over time. Heck, the day Dolly sold me this building for the cost of taxes had to have been key. It was from here that I'd solved mysteries from the past, and just today another began with a box covered in a petticoat from the country club's Golden Jubilee.

It didn't bear trying to figure out. I'd learned not to argue with the universe. I had wanted to say no to judging to begin with, so what does the universe do? It gives me the very dress I'd die to get my hands on. Smack in my lap, if I was lucky. Well, on a hanger, at least. And as long as I could get my hands on it, whether I picked it as a winner or not didn't matter.

Given the nature of the last, and possibly current, owner—if it belonged to the same person—I might not pick it on principle. Who needed a customer like Vainglory to try to satisfy?

I winced inwardly. Who was I kidding? I couldn't wait to get my hands on the peach gown and the tulle petticoats beneath it.

My fear? That would be the one dress not entered in the competition.

First things first. "When can I see the clothes?" I asked my moonstruck parents.

Fiona had the grace to look chagrined. She had no idea how long they'd zoned. They really needed me to get my own apartment.

She cleared her throat. "The entries are being delivered to you starting tomorrow, if not sooner."

"How did you know I'd say yes? Suppose I didn't want to judge?"

"You didn't," my father said, "but you caved. We knew you would. For us."

Fiona cuffed him.

"Let's just call it a mandate from the universe," I said, which made Fiona prepare to drag my father from the shop. We both knew it was better not to go there with him. I got thanked, kissed, and hugged extra hard before they left, since they'd duped me with manipulation aforethought.

"Hey!" I called after them. "Where did Eve go?"

"She had a class to teach," my father said. At UConn's Avery Point campus, where Dad himself taught.

Fiona chuckled. "Soon as we got you to the fainting couch, she ran out of here like she was being chased by a tall, open can of red paint."

For years, Eve wore only black, a palette which she had recently stretched to include dark earthy and metallic tones, after she'd tempered her wardrobe with a steampunky edge. Sure, I egged her on. So yes, a giant can of colored paint, any color, would scare her witless and turn her white as a cranky goose; that was a pun, Eve-style. "She's a wuss, my gothic friend."

"Yep, she is." Fee let my father work a bit to catch her hand as they crossed my parking lot, then she leaned into him to show she was teasing, and I heard his newly enlivened chuckle, a sound that had been absent for so long from our lives.

I waited to hear them drive away and then called the one

30

person who could tell me how the box had gotten into my attic. "Dante?"

No answer. No tuxedo-clad hunk appeared, top hat askew, wicked smile wide. "Dante, where are you?" My resident ghost, Dante Underhill, undertaker and Cary Grant clone, could not leave my building, formerly his building. He could however drive its new owner crazy. That would be me.

Not that I found him annoying. More like a perk. He kept me company and helped solve crimes. He watched over me and had saved me a time or three. He also hung around the women's dressing rooms with a big grin on his handsome face but, hey, nobody's perfect.

He made my days brighter and whispered sweet words of love . . . to his soul mate, Dolly Sweet, age 106, every time she stopped in. Almost daily.

Most times, Dante materialized when I called. This time, he did not. "I call your lack of attention guilt, my man," I said. "I'm betting you know something about that box. A tale you don't feel like telling. I also know that you're abandoning me on purpose, because you're stuck right here in this building for eternity."

I heard his charming chuckle. Felt the cool whisper of his hand on my cheek.

"Don't try to turn me up, sweet. Show or suffer."

Silence held. "That's it," I said, when he failed to show. "When I leave, I'm adjusting the electronic sound system. I'll blast the volume and fill each room with a different type of music. Hard rock. Jazz. Country and western. Rap. Disco."

Yes, Dante had gathered enough energy from my

customers over the past couple of years to move objects, open doors, and such. He could probably even turn an old Bakelite radio dial, but he had absolutely no control over electronics, or he hadn't figured them out yet. Either way, the lack drove him bonkers.

"When it's time for me to leave, no mercy!" I promised.

Tomorrow, after a night of dueling banjos, he'd squeal like a greased pig on a playground slide.

$\mathcal{F}ive$

I grabbed my yogurt from the mini fridge, because I'd long ago missed lunch. I must have spent more real time in the belly of that whale than I'd thought.

While I ate, I thought about Robin, who "they" said could swim through a stormy sea, and I wondered why she'd have to. I was afraid she'd tried to escape the person who'd "scavenged" her, or maybe she'd been pushed from a boat. I hated to think about how far her hunter had taken his role.

Part of me wanted to call the police or read the papers to see if the second best swimmer from Vassar had survived. But she'd gone into the water on that stormy night forty or more years ago.

I tried Googling her name and came up with links to thousands of red-breasted birds and pages of Celtic surnames. So much for that.

I bet the scavenger hunters never thought the box in my attic would ever come to light.

Their intentions had been almost honest in the beginning. They'd thought it was all being returned. Or most of them had. Whoever had inspired Robin to jump might have known better all along. Heck, abducting someone probably went above and beyond the terms of the hunt. And who were its missing members? The scavenger hunters, like slimeball and his ilk?

So many questions. What had happened to keep them from returning the box . . . which they'd put the scavenger list inside. I looked down at the box and shuddered to the point of rubbing the gooseflesh on my arms. "I will not open you alone. No way. No how. Wait! Where's the wrapper?"

I looked for Chakra, soother of my solar plexus, but she'd disappeared. "Chakra? Chakra baby?" I called. "I have a treat for you." Ba-da-bump, ba-da-bump, ba-da-bump. I heard her kitty paws running lickety-split on the hardwood floor, the sound of thumps getting dimmer, rather than louder. She wasn't running toward me but away. Had she stolen the petticoat piece that had given me my vision? "Naughty little furball!"

She growled an objection and scurried away, but she didn't return the goods.

I called Eve. "Hey, my goth computer-genius fact finder?"

"If that isn't a butter-up." Eve chuckled.

"I need names. Captains of the Vassar swim teams, range 1960 to 1973." Some of them might have graduated as recently as the June before the country club's anniversary event, which usually took place mid-summer.

"Madeira Cutler, are you sleuthing again? Never mind. I know the answer. It was that flipping box, wasn't it?"

"No, it was the fabric cover on the box, so there."

"Same thing," Eve said. "Anyway, you don't need a PIA Fed for that info. I'll get back to you in a blink." Click. She'd hung up. Must be teaching a class. Eve loved that Nick had sort of disappeared. She'd never liked him.

Now for my traitor of a cat. When I finally found Chakra, there wasn't a petticoat piece in sight. She swirled around my legs, purred, and even jumped into my arms and licked my knuckles to get back into my good graces, but she'd stashed the goods, all right.

"Chakra, I need that petticoat piece." I bit my lip. I should hand it over to Werner. It was absolutely, undeniably the biggest clue in a case of larceny gone horribly wrong. My visions were inadmissible, of course. And, well, Werner didn't know about my psychometric gift and wouldn't believe me if he did.

And he worked alone. I mean, if he were to have the fabric wrapper analyzed, I'd never know the story it told. Whereas, if I were to get it analyzed at FBI headquarters on the q.t., I would receive and understand the results, maybe piece them together with the vision. Of course, eventually I'd share the pertinent info with Werner, in my own way. But I was the only one—not counting the scavengers—who could give any new clues the chance of a correct spin.

Or maybe not. I dialed an old family friend, Tunney Lague, the local butcher, who not only cut the meat and sold it to you, he told you how to cook it so it tasted expensive and amazing. On the other hand, he also knew everything about everybody, mostly because he charmed the daylights out of them and lured their secrets out of them.

"Mad!" Tunney said as he answered his phone, and I could just see the handsome man—my father's age—standing there in his bloodstained apron, grinning. "You're looking good." He always said that over the phone.

"Tell me what you know about a scavenger hunt that might have taken place at the country club's fiftieth jubilee celebration."

Tunney whistled. "Nobody knows anything about that one, kid. An old friend of mine got mixed up in it. Drank himself to death but never spilled as much as a sentence as to what really happened, not even at his drunkest."

"Wow, if *you* don't know, who does?"

"Nobody, Mad. That's a closed case."

"Thanks, Tunney."

"Pork roast is on sale."

"I'll tell Aunt Fee."

"You do that. Bye, kiddo."

With no more info than I started with, I set my gloves beside me, sat near the box, and speed-dialed Nick, for like the millionth time since he left for DC. Nick has been my brother Alex's FBI partner for years.

All Alex knows now is that they're not partners anymore, that a bigwig showed up, asked Alex to step out of his and Nick's shared office, and spoke to Nick for a few minutes. Nick's eyes had widened as they spoke, Alex said. Then the bigwig led him away.

Alex told me Nick grinned and saluted him as he passed. That was their signal that everything was about to change.

And according to my brother Alex, Nick was happy about it. We're both pretty sure there was a promotion involved. Alex heard some scuttlebutt that a change of assignment, like maybe Europe, too.

Nick and I had always had a contingency plan in place, the FBI being what it was. Since I hadn't heard from him in five months, nearly six, three months being our cutoff date, we were currently in an off-again portion of our relationship. The longer the silence the more firm the breakup. Oh, Nick hadn't officially dumped me or anything. If he had, he would have told me—

"Paisley Skye answering for Special Agent Nick Jaconetti."

"Paisley, it's Madeira." Paisley had been my last client. Whaddaya know, I'd introduced my boy toy to a doll.

I heard whispers through the phone, which ticked me off a bit.

"Ladybug, what a surprise." Paisley had obviously been standing beside Nick. According to Paisley's great-aunt Dolly, Paisley had moved to France with her grandfather, Dolly's brother. "How'd the roof-raising go?" Nick asked. "Wasn't that today?"

If he remembered, he should have called. "All raised. Now I have to be patient while they finish the inside over the course of the winter."

"You don't know how to be patient."

"You leave me for months, no word, and you wanna talk about my roof, my impatience? Sticky subject right now." I stuck my tongue out at the phone for several not-so-childish reasons, and yet wasn't it about time we left high school behind us? I figured we could open the brass box of trouble together over the phone, as long as he was there to keep me calm. "Are you busy?" Besides with Paisley?

"That depends. Want to speak to a prime minister?" he whispered. "A defense minister? A four-star general? A dictator? Didn't Alex tell you I gave him the go-ahead when classified cleared."

I remembered the other night when my brother had really tried to get me to *sit still long enough for a talk.* Maybe I hadn't wanted to know.

"I think he's tried, but I've been too busy getting ready for the roof-raising. It doesn't happen without direction, you know."

"Well, Cupcake, they whisked me away for a slam-me-against-the-wall orientation with no outside communication, and then they took me out of the country."

"Without your consent?"

"I gave my consent years ago when I signed on for this gig. I'm unattached and an adventurer. You've always known that about me. I made that clear, right? You went to New York for seven years. Did I complain?"

"No, you forgot I existed." Like now. The silence, like the distance, between us grew.

"I want to see the world and climb the ladder at the same time. Haven't I always said that?"

Sigh. "Right." He had said it a time or three, and I'd ignored it, like when Alex's five-year-old, Kelsey, declared, "Someday I'm gonna be president."

"Well, get this, I've been promoted to attaché at one of the Bureau's classified liaison offices."

This time I embraced the knowledge pertaining to his

love of adventure though I wanted to break every bone in his body with that embrace. "Why you?" I asked. "Do I sound pouty?"

"Little bit," he said. "I forgive."

"The Paisley Skye case was bigger than any of us thought," Nick said. "She's working with us on it. Her family willed her their diaries, plus her grandfather has given his journal solely to her alone. So we need her."

Do we, now? "But Alex worked on Paisley's case with you. Why isn't he there?"

"Your brother eventually declined overseas promotions in his contract, because of Tricia and the kids."

I let silence carry my reply. I was thinking something along the lines of "What am I, chopped goose liver on a stale cracker?"

"Coming, sir," Nick said.

Great, I'd had my two minutes. Time was up.

"Cupcake. Werner's there for you, whatever you need," Nick added. "I trust him." Nick's phone dropped the connection.

Oh, I trusted Detective Sergeant Lytton Werner of the Mystick Falls Police Department, too, but we'd had a . . . thing, he and I, amounting to a personal best for thermonuclear kisses. A blip, yes—during another off period for Nick and me—but still an elephant in the room whenever Werner and I got together.

It was true, I could let down my guard with Werner in a way I couldn't with Nick. Be myself, no matter how wacko. Was it because I could leave high school behind with him? That he encouraged me to be me, showed he appreciated the mature Mad, the woman I'd grown into? To Werner, I might just be more than a booty call between international adventures. Maybe.

Inside, I was still processing. For Nick, I had already experienced most of the stages of grief, as it were. My roof-raising was a bit of reconstruction and a working-through, and after our short call I decided to work toward accep-tance and then hope for a new romantic future for myself.

In other words, get on with your life, Madeira Cutler. Easier said than done.

Though Nick did not say that he'd never be home . . . maybe it was time for me to grow up and move on from a relationship that never seemed to progress past a certain point. Again, I'd just have to work through it.

My second choice to have beside me when I opened the brass box: Detective Lytton Werner, with whom I liked feeling free to be me.

Maybe I didn't believe his acceptance would last, though. If that was the case I'd have to mourn later, but now I must move . . . onward and upward, like to my second-floor workroom to tackle a rack of alterations. From there I could see the surveillance camera's eye on the front door and hear the amplified sound of the bell above the door that heralded new arrivals. That way, I could design and sew during a quiet shop day.

I barely had a chance to get started.

The first set of gowns came within the hour. Aunt Fee delivered them and put them on racks, so I wouldn't inad-vertently get a reading.

She left quickly to return to my dad at the country club, where entries kept arriving. Wow, they'd really asked me last minute . . . so I wouldn't have time to change my mind, of course, the sneaky tacticians.

Hoping to see that particular gown from my trip to the past, I carefully unzipped each garment bag halfway down, until I had unzipped them all. Though I proved that many would fit the country club's *This Is Your Life* segment, I did not find Vainglory's gown among them, to my disappointment.

More disillusioned after my talk with Nick— something to think about—I went back to work.

Aunt Fee called around closing time. "Your father and I have put another batch of formals in garment bags. Can we bring them by? We feel as if we've accomplished something when we empty the room.

"You do. You give me the work."

Aunt Fee giggled, and not from my snarky comeback. "Is Dad standing beside you?"

"Oh . . . yes, and he said to tell you that he doesn't envy your task. And neither do I, sweetie. Though we know you well enough to know that you're going to love what you see."

"Bring 'em on." My heart raced at the thought. The possibilities. The opportunity . . . to read Vainglory's dress. I looked to the ceiling in petition. "If it please the universe."

Six

Dad and Aunt Fee arrived together with the second batch of formal wear, this one bigger than the first. And they placed these on a separate set of racks. "We think your mother was helping us this afternoon," Aunt Fee said.

"Either that," my dad said, "or one of these gowns has a pocketful of melted chocolate."

Aunt Fee and I groaned. My father winked. A measure of how far he'd come when it came to accepting the existence of the paranormal and the role of the women he loved within it.

After he ushered Fee out the door, I stood there among the garment bags while the scent of chocolate swirled around me. "Mom," I said. "You were helping them."

That scent was how my chocoholic mother made her presence known from the other side. My siblings—Sherry, Brandy, Alex—and I had discussed this chocolate nod from

Mom, and we decided that she made the rounds, swirling from one of us to the next, but that she stayed where she was needed most. We only wish we'd realized it as children.

So I put on my gloves and headed straight for the newest garment bags, unzipping the one indicated by a metaphoric chocolate arrow.

My heart flipped at my first look of peach tulle peeking from beneath the dress, and I wanted to get a good look at the gown before I hopefully "read" it, hence the gloves, so I removed its garment bag and put it alone on a separate rack, so that I could walk around it.

None of Fee's pictures did it justice. No doubt this was the dress. I knew that because the petticoat piece that had been wrapped around the box in my attic mimicked the gown's waist-high chevron design so perfectly, albeit in petticoat fabric, not satin. Plus, I'd seen Vainglory remove the petticoat from beneath her gown—this gown—and tear it into the pieces she distributed to her cohorts in which to hide their baubles—for years, as it turned out.

A fifties strapless gown of gathered dark peach tulle, it had a perfect heart-shaped bust and a Southern belle skirt with a hand-embroidered design that would also require a crinoline, or, as some designers called them, a cage.

Though there were certainly more expensive formals here, already this was unique. I'd attribute that to the cream satin apron appliquéd with two-inch, peach-and-white chevron stripes. They graduated in size depending on where they sat on the simple leaf-shaped back apron, which ended at the hips in back and at the waist in front. Its bib stitching mimicked the chevron stripes in a self fabric—forming a straight-up, single V—embracing the rib cage and raising the breasts to best advantage. The chevron stripes obliterated the waist seam. Such clean lines enhanced the figure.

This dress had been designed and worked by a master. I walked around it to the rear. One beauty of the apron was having it mirrored in the back, so that from the side you saw the petal skirts meeting about eight inches from the waist. A beauty from every angle, it had triplet chevron self-fabric bows down the back, a covered metal zipper, and a boned bodice.

I checked the inside of the bodice, making certain that no fabric touched my bare wrists in shorty gloves. I'd have to find some formal evening-length gloves for the future. They'd be best to keep me from getting a vision I did not want.

Not that it would be sane or work-efficient to wear gloves while fitting my customers. That would still be impossible, and I would still have to take that universal chance with my psychometric gift every time I did.

Inside, I found hand-stitched French seams and a label. Atelier, Liette de Paris, Originale. A private Parisian label by a designer of haute couture whose history and work I intended to study in the future.

As I suspected, the petticoats were missing. There should be a crinoline, or cage, closest to the body and at least four tulle petticoats above it. The one that had been destroyed would have been worn closest to the gown. Why did the petticoat and gown match? Because if the dress hem flipped up, say in a dance, the perfection of its beauty would be mirrored and enhanced, and not marred by a petticoat.

That most important piece of the formal had been

missing for more than four decades and just might hold the key to a murder, a detail I intended to confirm, if possible by reading the gown.

My cell phone rang before I had a chance, showing Eve as my caller. "Don't spare me the details," I said in lieu of a hello.

"I'm faxing you a list of Vassar swim captains as we speak. But this is a hoot. One of them was—"

"Sherry's mother-in-law?"

"Brat."

"If it's any consolation, I didn't know for certain. I knew that she went to Vassar, and something about the voice was familiar. Besides, a paper trail is confirmation, an actual clue, and admissible as evidence, except that my corroborating evidence is a psychometric trip to La La Land. It's still better than unfounded speculation, however."

"Damn, I have questions, but my next class is coming in."

"Wait, what year did she graduate?"

"Nineteen seventy-two. I'll want details, Cutler."

"I have to go read a gown now."

She hung up screaming, literally.

I chuckled as I took the gown.

I took it by the hanger to the fainting couch. Because when and if I zoned, there was always the possibility that I would also swoon, so I prepared for a soft landing.

Practically committing psychic hari-kari, I removed my gloves, laid the gown over me like a blanket, and wrapped my arms around it. The fabric was so soft; the imagery of its creation almost romantic.

Impatience got the better of me when I didn't zone in a

blink, and then I experienced a slight dizziness and disorientation, and, as I began to swirl away in earnest, Dante materialized—and about time. "I'm here for you," he said.

So I swirled away with a friend who would watch my back from the future. But suddenly, no friends stood among those on whom I would never turn my back.

I still held the treasure box that Vainglory had handed Bambi, shocked the gown had taken me back to the place I'd left, though I could have no idea what had transpired in my absence.

"Bambi," Grody said, "maybe you should take the scavenger list from the box before you give it back."

"Maybe she should." Vainglory chuckled. "But when? Tomorrow, next week, next year? It won't matter, really."

"What day is it?" Bambi asked.

"How much did you drink, girl?" Vainglory asked with a titter. "You know very well that we left the country club's Golden Jubilee dinner dance only a few hours ago."

"We've been out here more like ten or twelve hours, missy," Brut corrected. "It's got to be the day after by now."

It must be near dawn, I surmised, at which time I'd get to see their faces. My heart raced at the thought.

"Bambi-Jo, don't you think about writing any of this in one of your crazy journals or diaries," Vainglory stressed. "It didn't happen. Get it?" The depth of that threat did not go unnoticed by the others.

And then, deep in the back of my mind, Vainglory's voice came back to me, from around the time I had my first ever vision, with her uttering a different, more personal kind of threat to someone else. And with that, I believed that I could name her.

Oh, I could name her. I'd almost forgotten Eve's call. Zoning often totally separated me from the present, but not this time. I remembered.

I had been right. Vainglory was not just any woman, but her royal PIA self, a spoiled coed who would grow up to become my sister Sherry's witch of a controlling mother-in-law. I might not be able to prove much until the gown's first fitting in real time, when I might wheedle some answers out of her if I bowed, scraped, adored, and slobbered enough over her.

So Vainglory and Deborah VanCortland were one and the same poor little rich girl, who, as it turned out, happened to be the biological grandmother of my sister Sherry's twins, the poor things.

Biology aside, though the gown would flatter any figure, I suspected that Deborah may have outgrown it over the years. And shame on me for delighting in the thought.

Other than her size, she hadn't changed at all. Here, she'd been to an exclusive formal event—only the rich and greedy need apply—yet this coed and her cohorts had had to make their own fun, some of it off the tears of others.

That described Deborah to a T.

They were all bored rich kids, or, rather, adults, actually. Even I was guilty of according them young adult status, but not so according to their post-college comments. *Had been the best swimmer at Vassar.* Adults, yes. Deborah had been twenty-two or twenty-three at the time. Adults, and still they didn't get it. Somebody might have drowned tonight, and it seemed that most of them shrugged a mental "oh well."

No souls, these people.

"Why isn't Robin with us?" Bambi asked.

"She's more interesting to the guys than the rest of us at the moment," Vainglory said. "Not for any reason that I envy."

Bambi stamped a foot. "Can you speak English, please."

"You know," Vainglory stressed. "That trip to Paris Robin took last semester, for six months' worth of 'art lessons.' Really? I mean, trips like that, a girl usually leaves a little something behind . . ."

Bambi huffed.

I didn't sense that she caught Vainglory's "pregnant" pause but I knew when she gave up on getting an answer. "So why did she dive in the water? There's a storm for heaven's sake!" Bambi was either fearless or clueless, I wasn't sure which.

"What are you? A dimwit?" a new voice snapped. "Finishin' school din do you no good!" Wynona said. Lady Backroom, they called her behind her back—I somehow got that and her name straight from Bambi's thoughts. 'Cause finishin' school din do Wynona no good, neither, Bambi silently snapped.

Wynona was evidently a country-club tart who planned to marry rich, and when she got nervous, she forgot to act the lady.

Bambi did have some helpful musings, though I had to catch them as they bounced around her brain, like a zigzag stitch gone rogue.

"And we're not all here, ya twit," Wynona added. "Couple of the boys ain't. Probly doin' the deed to knock it off the list, the lucky stiffs." She tittered at her dubious joke.

It was like a time stamp, her phrasing. "Dimwit"—so not politically correct. Insulting and rude.

I did the math to see how long ago this event took place. The Mystick by the Sea Country Club was founded in 1923, which set their Golden Jubilee as happening in 1973. These people were all in their mid to late fifties to early sixties by now, like Odd Duck at the roof-raising, who, I'm betting, practically willed that box not to be found.

But how could I be sure? There'd been dozens of people that age in the crowd.

"How did we get into this mess?" asked Grody, who still pulled ambivalence from my every pore and twitched my ultrasensitive nerve endings raw. A sensible man, who at least knew they were in trouble, though maybe that was because he seemed to be at least five years older than the others. "All I did was join a country club," he said. "Dream of a lifetime, I thought, and now this. I mean, it was supposed to be a lark. A game of rascals and rogues, a scavenger hunt, and now what? I'll never make town selectman when this comes out. We could have a crime to hide. You all understand that, right?" he asked, though no one answered.

Well, he hadn't said "a crime to confess," so he wasn't as smart as I thought.

"I'm sorry," he said, "but I'll not be an accessory to . . . to—"

"You already are," Snake hissed, his threat palpable. "And the word you seek is 'murder.'"

Seven

It does not seem fair that, unbeknown to you, every single item you put on your body literally shouts out your unconscious dreams and desires to the entire world. Everyone who sees you can read you like a book, yet you yourself have no idea what you're saying.   —CYNTHIA HEIMEL

One of them produced a flashlight while they all ignored the word "murder" as if it had never been said, and wrapped their booty in petticoat squares like six prissy pirates, wily cohorts who looked more like escapees from a costume ball. Hard to believe that this happened before I was born. Not that I could see their formals clearly, but hooped skirts bounced against mine while tailcoats and striped cravats danced into and out of the shadows, an example of the sour cream of society.

Why did they linger in this dank place, mocked by the ripping tides that sounded closer by the minute, as if the ocean might devour them, which it appeared they deserved.

Had they been first to the scene of the actual crime, where Robin had been forced to take her swim? Or had they met here after that and heard the tale secondhand? How much was supposition? How much truth?

I wished I'd been in it from the beginning. I'd have had a clearer perspective. Crime or no crime? Which was it? Though their selfish acts and attitudes were crime enough.

So now they stayed, hiding away with their secret. I needed to know the why of it all before I turned back into a pumpkin, though the situation fit *Grimms' Fairy Tales* more than my own.

Bambi could identify them, but I couldn't force her to transfer that knowledge to me, or even to speak it, no matter how I willed her to. At the moment, I could put neither a real name or face to anyone but Deborah.

Of course, I knew Wynona as Lady Backroom. Fat lot of good that did me.

As I pondered it all, the flashlight illuminated a silver flask being wrapped in a piece of petticoat, but not before I saw blood smeared on the engraved flagon.

With that small bit of bobbing light, I caught bits of the people around me, parts of faces, even. Some could be related to current residents of Mystic and its environs, I suppose, and though Deborah's voice rang familiar, I barely recognized her. She was a full forty years younger than the last time I'd seen her. One for the books.

They concentrated on their wrapping, the better to hide their deeds, but in shadow I saw the nebulous man, tall, gangly, all lines and angles. Snake gestured as he spoke, and I recognized him as the one who had the barest trace of a Southern accent. A trait that sailed in and out of his speaking voice, as if he was trying to overcome it but failed when agitated.

Snake took it upon himself to grab pieces of that petticoat and hand them round to his so-called friends. "Hide your prizes well for now," said he. "Every piece has to be returned to its proper owner."

"When?" Bambi asked.

Vainglory huffed, clearly miffed. "Bambi-Jo, you just don't know when to shut up."

I sensed the strength of Bambi's dislike. Whaddaya know, we had something in common. Two things: She wanted facts, too, and she didn't like Deborah much, either.

"But when?" Bambi asked again louder, stronger.

"When we see what the tide brings in," Snake snapped, claiming the role of leader. "Which reminds me," he added. "Don't throw the scavenged items you're responsible for in the drink. The sea has a way of returning what we don't want, and if just one borrowed item comes back with a body, we're done for."

"What body?" Bambi asked again, so they all looked at me, or her, like we had two heads—I guess we did. Two brains that thought alike, anyway. I thought I might try to find Bambi first, after I returned to the present—kindred spirits, her and I.

I might know her well enough to inspire her to talk. I'd contact her, if ever I escaped this boat-belly place.

Yes, that was beginning to worry me, how long I was staying this time around. Vainglory's gown had big mojo, but then, it belonged with the petticoat, which had been splintered and traveled far with the help of Deborah/Vainglory, Brut, Wynona, Grody, Snake, and even Bambi-Jo, which wouldn't make my investigation any easier.

"I don't like that we can't find Robin," Bambi said.

Snake snorted. "You didn't like her any more than we did."

He spoke of Robin in the past tense, I noted, and Bambi didn't deny it.

Snake, with his peekaboo accent, shouldn't be too hard to track down, if he was still alive.

"The scavenger hunt was your idea," he reminded Bambi. "And when did you grow a conscience?"

"Screw you. I started with a tame inventory of pretty baubles. That added list of unsavory conquests was your idea. I told you those things could harm people."

Snake waved a defiant piece of petticoat at her.

She grabbed it and gasped. "Where did the blood come from?"

"I cut myself on a broken window getting in." He showed the cut across his wrist.

"I cut myself, too," said Grody, further mixing my emotions. Would Robin's body show signs of trauma?

It took two of them to climb across broken glass before one had the sense to open a door? They lie.

"What if Robin doesn't make it back to shore?" Bambi cried, working herself into a good case of hysteria. "What do we do then?"

"The body will do what a body does," Snake said without a care, as if offering us mint juleps from a porch swing by a peach tree, miles away from Mystic, and years away from the present, which is where I was heading.

Eight

The mind is like a richly woven tapestry in which the colors
are distilled from the experiences of the senses, and the
design drawn from the convolutions of the intellect.

—CARSON MCCULLERS

After work, I prepared to visit Werner at the police station
without the fabric the brass box had been wrapped in. It
seemed that Chakra had absconded with the original covering, and I hadn't yet found her hiding place. What a
cheeky kitty. She really had a thing for tulle. With a place
full of sixties and seventies gowns, she was in turn accost-
ing and "making love to" anything tulle in the shop. That
was some estimable quantity, yet none got left un-fooled-
around-with. She wasn't harsh. She didn't tear anything.
She rolled, she wallowed, she purred, as if they were all
made of catnip. And if a tattered piece fell off from too
much cat-love, she ran with it, and it got secreted away for
her later rolling pleasure. They'd be lucky to get a print off
the original box-covering when Chakra was done.

To turn Werner up sweet and distract him from the

missing fabric cover, I changed into a fifties Mainbocher three-piece linen blend suit in a cheery citron. I particularly loved the jacket's wide-cut double-notched collar and pearlescent cream Lucite buttons. Mainbocher is probably best known for designing the wedding gown and trousseau for Wallis Simpson's 1937 wedding to Edward VIII, the Duke of Windsor.

I confess that I dressed well to sweeten the detective's mood, in a business suit sort of way. But I countered my sobriety of choice with a pair of Giselle, Lady Double You "Giselle" spikes in buckskin tan suede, with bronze hand-applied metallic leather crests from ankle to heel tips. Nothing shows off a leg better than giving it wings.

I reapplied my makeup while I enjoyed the beat of a big band piece called "Don't Sit under the Apple Tree (with Anyone Else but Me)."

Too late for you, Jaconetti, I thought. You made your choice.

Why, when I was on my way to see Werner, did I feel giddy? Why did the universe wag that jazzy finger my way? Like I should embroider a scarlet letter on my blouse for moving on with my life? Sheesh. I'd recovered from the shock of losing Nick, made peace with his decisions, especially when he had Paisley with him. Now I was free to make some choices of my own.

I topped the outfit with the tiniest forties ochre satin twist toque labeled: Balenciaga, 10 Avenue, George V Paris.

Not until after I'd donned my supple kid gloves did I place the recovered country club treasure box into an appropriately sized Vuitton travel bag that matched my personal shoulder bag. and wished I had Chakra's petticoat scrap.

At the police station, Officer Billings saluted and grinned when he saw me. "Gad, ma'am, I sure hope the detective stops yelling now that you're around again."

"I'm not moving in," I said. "And you can drop the 'again.'"

"Sorry to hear that, ma'am. He's not here, anyway. He took the late shift last night so a couple guys could go to a bachelor party. He's working from home today."

"Will you do me a favor? Call Detective Werner and ask him if I can drop by?"

The desk clerk made the call and set the phone on speaker.

I winced, preparing for Werner's shout, but even when we were frenemies, I'd liked him, though I'd kept expecting the grizzly to show his claws.

"Not her again," Werner grumbled.

I raised my arms because he'd repeated the "again," but I could tell that the Wiener didn't mean it. Have I mentioned that I dubbed him that in third grade?

Picture it: The Cafeteria. Lull in the conversation. When he poked the tiger—that would be me—I called him "Little Wiener," instead of Lytton Werner, so the whole school heard it together. And it stuck . . . to this day.

Surprising how many times the words "Wiener" and "again" had popped up since I walked in the door to the station.

"Good," I said. "Thanks. I'll be right over, er, unless you're otherwise occupied."

"Madeira, when I say I'm working at home, I'm working."

Funny, I thought I remembered an occasion when he/we weren't quite. "Working," that was.

When I pulled into the drive, Werner opened his front door, not the kitchen door I used to breeze through without knocking. Putting up a wall. Testing formality as its fabric. Self-protection, however weak.

Never mind. I could knock down all his defenses with a pair of well-placed innocently lowered lashes. I needed the Wiener on my side today.

Standing there waiting for me, he made a show of rolling down his sleeves and slipping into his suit jacket to prove this was business.

Point taken, but I so wanted to keep him as a friend, frenemy, ally . . . as a pair of arms I could step into? Hmm.

He left the door open for me and disappeared, and when I got inside, I found him in his home office, behind a desk bigger than the one he used at the station.

All business.

In the doorway, I raised my shoulders and lowered them again. Did I look innocent enough? What could I say, except: "I brought a peace pipe."

I stopped across the desk from him, almost at attention. If the words "peace pipe" made him think about us while we played the Indian lovers Running Bear and Little White Dove—an intimate rock and roll encounter during a previous sleuthing expedition of mine—well, so be it. It was a good memory that I did not want to lose.

He tilted his head, and I guessed that was the most positive response I could expect, given the circumstances. We hadn't talked much, if at all, since Nick and I got back together. And I'd missed this special old friend, but I couldn't tell him that.

Not that I'd actually dumped him. We were never an item. We'd just had some . . . special events . . . together. Memorable ones. When Nick and I became godparents to my sister Sherry's twins, my family sort of pushed us together. It suited for a while, until Nick practically lobbied his way into feeding his adventure bug . . . again.

"Again," I said. *I'm ba-ack*, I did not say.

Since I couldn't seem to give our memories, including one thermonuclear kiss, the slip stitch, I kept them shoved deep at the back of my mind and rarely took them out to examine.

"We both know the past is the past," I said, and he nodded. "But the future holds promise. And our taste buds don't change." I pulled a Dos Equis from a recyclable shopping bag and set one bottle in front of him, one in front of me. This, too, came from yet another previous sleuthing experience we shared. One of our earliest ones.

His eyes brightened, but his fists clenched. Fighting with himself. "I'm not supposed to drink on the job," he said, sotto voce.

"It's after six, and I'd think working from home should have some perks. Besides, did I hear a no?"

I cupped the back of my ear. "No?" I saluted. "I'm looking for a negative, Detective, sir!"

He gave me a half smirk, and with a satisfied nod I shut his blinds.

He raised both brows.

"So people don't see you drinking on the job."

He flipped on the desk lamp, and I hung the jacket of my

dress in the room's closet, since he made his "office" in a main floor bedroom.

When I turned back to him, he'd already tipped back his bottle, his throat working convulsively.

"That's a mighty thirst," I teased. Mighty fine throat work, too. Oh, oh.

"Sweet," he said, eyeing me.

"The beer?" I asked. Or me? Okay, Cutler, stop flirting. He's more than a rebound guy, he's a friend. Don't use Werner to punish Nick. But the truth was, I meant every word. Myself. I was being nothing but myself.

"The hat," he said, rising and indicating the chair across from him.

I nodded. "I thought you'd make fun of the one with the feather."

"I would have." He didn't sit until after I did, and even then he watched me with speculation for a bit too long to be comfortable.

I sat and clutched my gloved fingers before me on the desk—a nervous, guilty giveaway—and to make matters worse, I leaned forward as if this were just between us. I guess I was doubly skittish. Hiding evidence—sort of, maybe—and seeing my not-quite-ex again, one-on-one, empty house and all that. Was he my ex? Yeah. Imagine that.

This would have been more professionally played at the station. I sighed and jumped in with both aerodynamic feet. "What if I might have evidence of a crime?" I asked.

Werner sat back, picked up his beer, and waited.

"If I gave you the evidence, would you let me help you solve the crime?"

"If? Ever hear the phrase 'obstruction of justice'?"

I copied his posture to the letter. "If there was a crime," I said, leaning back in my chair a bit, "the statute of limitations has long run out on the scenario I have in mind."

"Some investigations warrant being reopened," he said.

"What if an incident was neither recognized as a crime nor investigated in the first place?" I wasn't talking about the seemingly obvious robbery of the country club. I had other pleats to fold, like throwing him off the scent with the scavenger hunt, and then looking for a talented team swimmer from Vassar named Robin. *Oh! I should ask Eve if she can find Deborah's swim team listed anywhere. Maybe they won a meet, a championship, something to get them listed in a newspaper. I needed Robin's last name.*

"What do you have up your sleeve?" He rubbed the stubble on his chin, a whole day's worth of five o'clock shadow. He hadn't bothered to shave this morning.

I liked his big-bad-bear look. Dicey news for my currently muddled and crush-like mindset. "Does it look like I could hide anything in these tight sleeves?" I asked.

"Speaking of tells." He took a quick, imperceptible inventory from my winged heels to my tease of a toque. His gaze slid once up. Once down. Then he folded his arms. "You think you know how to distract me."

"This suit is from the fifties, though the pencil skirt is too tight for rock and roll. I'll admit," I said, "I'm aware that you like to see a girl in a skirt more than slacks. You once demonstrated your reasons quite well. I chose the outfit in hopes of sliding us past our, well, past"—best not make it "torrid past"—"and putting us at ease during a business discussion." I tilted my head. "And maybe I wanted to dredge up a memory or two, the playful ones. So sue me."

He made a sound fit for a grumpy grizzly. "And maybe you want to get back at Nick for putting his Mystick Falls house up for sale."

I actually felt the color drain from my face as I gripped the side of Werner's desk. "His house is for sale?"

Sir Galahad to the rescue. He handed me his bottle of Dos Equis, because mine wasn't open yet. I took a thirsty swig and let him hold a wet towel to the back of my neck. "I could kick myself for letting that one out of the bag," he said.

"How long's it been for sale?" I asked, eyes closed. "He just told me this morning that he'd left the country."

"I thought you were building the third-floor apartments because you knew—"

"Weeks? I've been prepping construction for weeks— Nick's known for weeks?"

"You were so happy about raising your roof. Maybe he didn't want to—" Werner raised his arms in defeat. "I am stepping away from this. Talk to your brother, Alex."

I patted my brow and cheeks with the cool cloth, gently so as not to lose my makeup. "I will. Thanks. I don't suppose you'd like to dance a little rock and roll, get me out of this slump?"

"With you on the rebound? No way."

"See, I only suggested that to make you smile, and you grumped instead."

Werner resented his half smile. I could tell. "I remember our rocking and rolling," he said. "It was fun. All of it."

He sat, slapped his hands on his desk, and pushed himself up, tossed his bottle in the trash, and opened the blinds.

I got it. He'd just put period to any kind of intimacy between us, especially the sharing of memories.

"What's your game, Mad?"

"I called Nick, and found him on the other side of the world, because I . . . need help. You know what he said? That you would be here for me if I needed you. He trusts you to be my go-to guy."

Werner grumped again, looked out the window, put his hands behind his back. "Your Fed's not as smart as I thought."

"He's not my Fed anymore. We're off again." I neatened Werner's desk a bit, moved anything tippy aside, then I set the travel bag between us.

"What's in there?" he asked, turning.

"I have no idea. I didn't want to open it alone."

Still standing, he peeled the Vuitton's soft leather top back to reveal its contents, engraved plate facing his way. I grabbed Eve's camera by its straps from my shoulder bag and snapped a pic. "I'd like to report a robbery," I said, proud to sidestep Werner's misgivings and my rocky start to rewinning his trust, because I suddenly knew he mattered more than I realized. "I'd like to enter this into evidence."

"A cash box?"

"I don't know. Like I said, we found it today when—"

"I heard."

"You let me squirm all this time and you knew we found something in my attic?"

"I like watching you squirm, a rather entertaining sport.

Your rare insecurity. . . charms me. Makes me feel manly. I wanted a minute to savor. Congrats on the third floor, by the way."

He liked watching me wriggle? What a stinker, but I couldn't tell him so if I wanted his help. "I'll be glad when it's done so I can move in."

"You're leaving your father's?"

"Dad and Aunt Fee need to be alone at her house. Alex is buying the old Cutler tavern."

Werner's range of expressions morphed three times fast: pleased, wistful, blank. And in a blink, blank won. "I used to expect you and Nick to set up housekeeping."

I barked a laugh. "Not our style, especially when we live in different countries."

The silence ran long, the pounding of my heart echoing in my head. My cheeks warmed to a blaze.

Werner's lack of opinion—while I could imagine what it might be—forced me to admit that my relationship with Nick, especially our living arrangements, shouldn't be up for discussion. Not now. Especially not with this man, who held a strong jolt of power over me.

What mattered is that Nick and I were off again. He was selling his house. Why did that make me feel less like a loser and more like a winner? I suddenly felt . . . free? Wholly so.

Really? Free to do what? Was I so flighty that I couldn't commit? Why did I care that I couldn't? Because of what Lytton Werner thought of me?

He opened his drawer for a cigar, caught my disapproving eye, and threw it back. "No Commitment Maddie, that's you."

"Scrap!" I focused sharply on his face. "Don't go there."

"You're right," he said. "I don't think either of us is ready for the truth here."

And what did that mean?

Nine

"The time has come," the Walrus said,
"To talk of many things:
Of shoes—and ships—and sealing wax—
Of cabbages—and kings—"
—LEWIS CARROLL, *THROUGH THE LOOKING-GLASS
AND WHAT ALICE FOUND THERE*

"Your new apartments," Werner said, bringing us back to the subject at hand and out of the danger zone.

"Right. I'm really excited about them. I'll put the other two up for lease and become a landlady. Dolly's talking about taking one. She says Ethel stifles her sex life."

Werner choked and opened the beer sitting in front of me. After he took a long sip and caught his breath, he grinned. "I want to be her when I grow up—the male variety, of course. Most hundred-and-six-year-olds can't utter the word 'sex.'"

He gave me a swift peek at the lady-killer grin I'd been missing without realizing it.

I grabbed another cold beer from the bag, took the cap off, and touched it to my warm cheek. "Me, too. Exactly like her." Out of nowhere, we clicked bottles. A truce, and

I didn't know which of us had instigated it. Must have been spontaneous, which often gets us into trouble.

Holy zipper foot, I so needed his kind of trouble.

"Why do you think this was stolen?" His question, as he perused the brass box found in my attic, took us to safer ground.

I scoffed. "You think somebody bought it from the country club and hid it in my attic for several decades?"

"You have a point," he said. "But what makes you think it was there for decades?"

"If it didn't get left there the night the body drawers got ransacked, it has to be decades. Because I haven't had a break-in since I bought the building except for that one incident, and even then it wasn't a break-in as much as a walk-through. I mean the place was wide open. Any way to find out how often Dolly's unoccupied building was broken into over the years? Or if it was burglarized when it was a funeral parlor–carriage house or before that when it was the old county morgue?"

Werner hit a few keys on his computer, which sat on a table that formed an L off his desk, to move from his document to an official-looking legal database that needed a password. Once in, he checked what looked to be a national register. "No break-ins on record back to around 1985, when we first got computerized."

He hit speed dial on his phone. "Billings, send an officer down to the old records room to check Mad's building in all its incarnations. See if and when it's ever been broken into. If ever, how many times, dates, and details, please."

I bit my lip. "You're right. It could have been put there anytime since 1923, when the country club opened." Not true, strictly speaking, but Werner didn't know that it had been stolen the night of the country club's Golden Jubilee. "It could have happened when either Dante or his father was in charge."

Werner looked up from his computer. "Dante?"

Werner doesn't know about my psychometric gifts, that my mother was a witch, or that the late Dante Underhill, undertaker, had been cursed to live in his carriage house—aka my shop—for eternity. Which meant that he didn't know I could talk to Dante the ghost, either, or that Aunt Fiona could, as well as Dante's old flame, Dolly Sweet, age 106. Good thing we weren't a couple, Werner and I. I'd have a lot of 'splainin' to do.

"Dante's one of the former owners of my building. The undertaker Underhills. Dante, the son, took over after his father passed." I tried to look innocent, realizing I shouldn't act so familiar with a dead man. "Dante's the one who died young and took the Underhill line with him, left Dolly his fortune and his building. And she sold the building to me . . . and told me all about him." There, that should explain my knowledge.

"Ah," Werner said. "I remember now. Dolly's infamous secret love affair . . . which everybody knew about."

I chuckled. "That's the one. I'm always finding papers with his signature. Upstairs, some of the open struts have his name carved in them. I think he hung around upstairs at the funeral chapel–carriage house as a kid, with a jackknife. He'd carved the horse stalls, too, before they became my dressing rooms. Sometimes, I think I can hear the young Dante playing tic-tac-toe with a friend on the raw wood upstairs."

Werner sort of grunted. Then he slipped on a pair of

latex gloves to examine the box. "Why don't you know what's in it?"

"I wanted a witness as to what's inside when I opened it, but before we try, I'd like permission to take pictures of whatever we find."

"I don't see why not, unless it's a secret map to the Federal Reserve bank. The average ordinary shop owner would have kept this, you understand, and kept her mouth shut, à la finders keepers."

"I'll take that as a compliment."

"It's not that you're extraordinary, Mad, just weird."

"Thanks." I wondered if that was to establish our nonromantic relationship up front.

Werner pushed the box my way, and I had this ticked-off urge to pick it up and hit him over the head with it.

Werner's eye twinkle said he could read me better than I thought, so I closed my expression and tried to blank my mind.

He'd love causing me a good pout. I wouldn't give him the satisfaction.

"Go ahead," he said, gruff, annoyed, probably because he could no longer read me. "Open her up."

"Okay." At first, the contents didn't surprise me, stacks of hundred dollar bills, most quite crisp and with dates that probably gave us a better bead on the year. I'd actually thought of it as a cash box a time or two.

I lifted the back bin, where checks were usually stashed in typical cash boxes, though most such boxes weren't made of brass. "This one must have been specially crafted for them," I said. "Ack. No check, but I found a couple five hundred dollar bills back here. It's U.S. currency, I think, dated in the forties. Oh, and beneath is a one thousand dollar bill; a red one. They must be forgeries. What have we stumbled on?"

He handled the odd bills, examined them, held them under the light, and I went around the desk to examine them as closely.

"They might be real," he said, looking at me. "I believe that the U.S. had legal tender in those denominations once."

"How do you know?"

He looked at me like I asked a lame knock-knock joke. "Degree in law enforcement?"

"Oh, you mean, like, Forgery 101?"

"That's about the scope of it."

The smallest bills in the box were fifties, but there weren't many, and I had to remove an antiqued brass tube about the size of the bills to get to them. But the small box inside the cash box turned out to be more interesting than the bills. It was outlined in—rubies, I believed, not garnets—on the outside, with a second row of sapphire chips to make a double dotted line around the outside top of the box. I lifted the cover on the pricey container, though where it was hinged made it more of an oblong box than a tube.

I caught my breath when I saw what it held, not that I saw the object, because it was wrapped in a petticoat piece, a much smaller one than I already had.

Both of us still wearing gloves—and a good thing—I removed the fabric wrapping, which did the job that tissue might have in protecting the object, and I gasped.

Werner whistled. "Is that real?" he asked.

I ran my gloved finger over the small, flawless shoe, covered in what appeared to be diamonds. It had a flat top that started at the vamp, extended to the top of the heel, and overlapped the slightest bit at the back. I lifted the overlap and saw the shoe was hollowed out. "Is this a snuffbox?"

Werner appeared flummoxed. "It sure looks like one. Those can't be diamonds covering it," he said. "No matter how real they look."

"If they're not," I said, "they're better than the best fakes I've ever seen. And the weight. Here, hold it. Feel how heavy it is."

He held the snuffbox in his palm and tested its weight. "You once said you knew diamonds," he pointed out.

I remembered the case and the victim.

"Our belief systems can be tested," I admitted. "I'm not as smart as I once thought I was."

"I think our Maddie's maturing into Madeira."

"Don't tell my father, or anyone else for that matter, if you think you like my real name."

Werner shook his head. "Given the dates and sizes of those bills, I'd say the dazzle on this snuffbox is more than likely to be diamonds."

"What's it made of inside that's weighing it down?"

"First guess? Lead," he said.

I set it down.

"Or," he added, "solid gold. Something ripe for fencing."

"If this is pure solid gold, never mind the diamonds—" I raised a brow. "In today's market, it's a new house."

"We may be looking at a case of first-degree larceny."

"What's the difference between theft and larceny?"

"Here in Connecticut? The difference is in the value of the items taken. If those are diamonds, and that's not a wooden shoe with a weight in it, our thief is a felon."

Werner didn't know the worst of it, like a possible death

by drowning, aka murder, but I didn't know yet if Robin had gone missing that night or made it to shore.

Seam rippers and pin tucks, I was ashamed that I didn't even know Robin's last name.

"How much money do you think is in the box?" I asked.

"Count it," Werner said, his fingers flying over the computer keys. "Wait. Found something here."

"Read it out loud."

"Looks like a cash box was stolen from the cloak room during the country club's twenty-fifth anniversary, or Silver Jubilee."

I shook my head. "You mean the Golden Jubilee."

He raised his hands from the keyboard, turned on the wheels of his I'm-the-boss chair—so big, it doubled as a throne—and looked down at me like I might be a lowly peasant. "Madeira? What makes you so sure it was the fiftieth?"

I scrounged for an answer that made sense. "Ah . . . that piece of fabric." Like the one the box was wrapped in and I lost, I did not say.

Whew. He bought it.

What do experts on body language call an instantaneous reaction, the look that escapes before one can school one's thoughts? Micro expressions, that's it. And it was too late to pull mine back; I knew it had been filled with shock to hear about the twenty-fifth.

"Madeira Cutler, what do you know that I don't?"

Oh. He didn't buy it after all.

Ten

Only self-appreciation is allowed in the fitting room. Praise
your curves and give thanks for those fantastic legs.
—JANIE BRYANT, *THE FASHION FILE*

The twenty-fifth anniversary of the Mystick by the Sea
Country Club did not compute, according to my vision.
Unless, as I stood in Bambi's shoes, I had not been given
the same box my construction boss found in my attic, but I
assumed it was the very same, because it sent me there.

Could the cash box I was given have been a different
one? Or had the box in the belly of the whale been stolen at
the twenty-fifth, and, ah, perhaps re-stolen on the country
club's fiftieth? Was taking the cash box some kind of gen-
erational privilege, a rich, entitled-family tradition? Theft,
really?

Surely computers would put period to the possibility of
stealing a cash box at the centennial at least. People would
pay by credit. So why didn't they at the fiftieth in 1973?
Surely credit cards were in use, though I remember Dad
saying once that "the average Joe" didn't start abusing

them until the early eighties. Then again, people who belong to country clubs aren't average Joes, are they? They would have been using Diners Club cards since the fifties. But my dad's generation was likely too smart to fully embrace the death of solvency. Perhaps.

"Madeira, I'm waiting for an answer."

I sighed. "Scavenger hunts, real ones, were tradition, weren't they, in the old days? Passed down from one generation to the next? A rite of passage? Maybe that same box was stolen repeatedly—"

Werner tilted his head like I might have grown horns. "With the same old money in it?"

"That doesn't compute, does it? That way it isn't stealing, is it, if you don't spend the money?"

Werner went to his window to look out toward the Mystic River. "It's still stealing, if you keep it."

"Right, and if it was tradition, it might be stored for that very purpose."

"Too valuable," Werner said. "The large bills are old enough to have been used at the country club's opening thousand-dollar-a-plate event. Or maybe it was five hundred dollars a plate back then, and somebody paid for two dinners with the thousand dollar bill?"

I got up to cross the room, open the closet, and get a mint from my jacket pocket. Stalling for time. Showing off my legs, giving Werner a look at the wings on my Giselle, Lady Double You spikes.

I walked back to the desk, remembered what Snake said about the scavenger-hunt list, and wondered if it was still inside the box. Without a word, I started counting the money. Werner came over to help. I lifted the back box that covered the $500 and $1,000 bills. Nervous, I fumbled it, and the whole brass box ended up on the desk upside down.

That amused Werner, seeing me flustered. "What's with you?" he asked.

What I thought I knew and who I thought I wanted were toying with my psyche. "Oddly enough," I said, putting down another stack totaling a thousand dollars, "I think I know why I presumed it was taken from the country club's fiftieth. Dad and Aunt Fiona are chairing the country club's *This Is Your Life* segment of the Very Vintage Valentine fund-raiser."

"And?"

"I'm picking five formals that were worn to the Golden Jubilee to see whose life will be read. My bad. I guess I had the Golden Jubilee on my mind."

Werner hadn't managed to count all the money, but he'd thrown it all in evidence bags. Also, each in its own evidence bag, were the shoe-shaped snuffbox, the sapphire-and-ruby-studded box it came in, and the piece of petticoat that had wrapped it.

"What are you doing with that?" I asked, referring to the petticoat piece.

"Bagging it as evidence?"

"Really? An old piece of cloth?"

"We don't ignore a hair at a crime scene. You know that."

I did know it, and my conscience was killing me. "I guess I thought of it as being like . . . tissue paper. Tossable. Didn't think of the box as a crime scene, either. Guess that's why you're the detective." Did I sound dumb or what?

"You reported the robbery, Mad. What's with you?"

"That tissue-like piece of fabric reminds me of an outfit I have at the shop. Can I borrow it for tonight, to compare? I'll give it back to you tomorrow, and it won't have been touched by human hands." Only kitty paws, if I lost sight of my crazy cat. And if I didn't lose sight of her, I might find her original stash. I actually wanted the new piece as bait. Cat bait.

"If it was anybody else," he said, "I'd be suspicious. Anyway, evidence is evidence, and don't you forget it."

I huffed. "It's not like you don't know where to find me, or think I'm gonna skip town. Pick it up on your way to work tomorrow."

"I have the weekend off, unless there's an emergency. But Monday morning, first stop, the country club. I mean, this has been missing a good many decades, I think it can wait until Monday."

"Can I go to the country club with you?"

"No, but I'll come by your place afterward, tell you how it went."

I resisted huffing a second time. "It's not like it's big enough for me to whip up an outfit with," I grumbled, entertaining him, I saw, so I shut up. Then my mind clicked back into gear. Son of a stitch! Now that the cash box was empty, I realized there was no scavenger-hunt list inside.

"What's that?" Werner asked, pointing into the interior of the empty cash box.

"Nothing. What?"

He lifted the separators out in one piece and ran his hand over the bottom. Then he grabbed a letter opener from a pencil cup and gently scored the inside edges of the cash box, until a corner of the paper bottom came up.

"Hey, I didn't notice that."

"Stick with me, kid."

We both ignored the echo of those fateful words, the yearning in them, as he slipped the opener beneath the paper bottom, all along the edges, then deeper under until the false bottom lifted up and out.

"It's in three pieces," Werner said, and we laid them out then moved them around like a puzzle.

"Yes! The scavenger-hunt list." It proved that the cash box was also related to the fiftieth anniversary, as I'd guessed earlier, which might not be a good thing. One of these days Werner would realize that I know too much too soon.

One of these days, maybe I should tell him . . . everything.

Unable to do that at the moment, however, I picked up all three pieces of the list.

" 'Golden Jubilee Scavenger Hunt,' " I read. "Wow, look at the things they listed to scavenge: 'Cane/walking stick. Double points if the walking stick's got a blade, firearm, or a flask inside. An engraved flask; double points if it's full. An antique inkwell, a copper-dipped baby shoe' . . ." I ran my hand down the list. "Oh, and here at the bottom, an antique snuffbox. I'll bet the thief didn't even know what that particular one could be worth," I added.

Werner took the list from my hand. "There's a point value for each item, including the cash box," he said. "And get this, scrawled at the bottom—we'll have to have the penmanship analyzed, and the paper dated, and checked for prints—'let a pet loose, set a boat adrift, move a car to the beach, entice a spouse not your own from the dance, a hundred points.' " Werner whistled.

I took the list back. " 'Kiss someone else's spouse, five hundred points'? 'All the way with someone else's spouse, five thousand points.' " I gasped. "All the way?"

"I presume you know what that means," Werner deadpanned.

Enough to know why Robin might dive into a stormy sea—if her enticer was going for the five thousand points. If she fought him on it, that might be the way Snake or Grody got bloodied up. "Sick game."

"The people who joined this particular scavenger hunt were thieves and worse," Werner said.

"I just can't believe they all agreed to it."

"Peer pressure's a bitch, and who all are you talking about?" Werner asked. "You act like you know them."

"Whoever went along with it," I said. "I mean, if I ended up with that cash box in my building, people actually did go along, didn't they?"

I sat across from Werner once more. "So, it didn't get stolen from the country club's twenty-fifth jubilee, hey? It says the fiftieth at the top, right? But that red thousand dollar bill has to be from as far back as the twenty-fifth. Do you think they re-steal the box every anniversary? Maybe stealing the cash box is like a symbol of the event. Maybe somebody so rich they didn't care what was in it, kept the box and passed it down from father to son to keep the tradition alive. Too far-fetched?" I asked.

"I still think it's fishy that you were right," he grumbled, scrolling down his computer page of information and reading further. "Okay, here we go. Assorted items are stolen from the club and its guests regularly, but they're usually returned. A stupid rich-people ritual."

"Can you pull the files on the country club thefts from that far back, for us to peruse?" I asked.

"Joining the force, Ms. Cutler?"

"C'mon, Lytton. I brought you the box. I didn't play finders keepers. You know what a good sleuth I am. I could help you."

"You could distract me."

"Really?"

"Don't pretend you don't know how beautiful you are when you flirt to get your way. It's the thing I like best and least about you."

"Depending on?" I asked.

"Whether you and Nick are on again or off again."

"Off," I said nonchalantly. "Thanks. I think. And by the way, no woman ever thinks she's beautiful. I can list my flaws for you if you'd like."

"No need. I'm sure I can list them myself."

"Gee, thanks." Like what? I wondered. Mousy hair, problem skin, knobby knees, big feet.

"Ma-dear-ra, hell-lo-oh?"

"Uhm, what?"

"Where'd I lose you? Or to who?"

"I was trying to solve the case. Like . . . why would they hide that box in my building and forget about it, if they planned to steal it again at the next anniversary?"

"That's why we investigate."

"We? You're going to let me help?" I reached for him then lowered my arms. "I can't thank you enough."

He regarded the evidence bags all over his desk, picked up the phone, and called Billings to come and get them. "You could thank me enough. We'll discuss how later."

Urp.

"You can be my silent, invisible partner."

Bummer. "So let's do some more research. Have there been any other juicy happenings at any other country club events? A catfight or cockfight? Somebody steal somebody else's porch swing?" Toss somebody in the ocean?

"Yes. Before you distracted me, I found an actual scanned police report, here, from 1973, about a minor who stole her mother's Parisian gown, insured at half a million dollars. But most of it was returned."

"Most of it?"

"Missing petticoat, worth a paltry seventy-five thou, though losing it reduced the value of the ein-sum-blech. That's a quote. Stupid word."

He pronounced "ensemble" with entertainment value, so I chuckled on cue.

He looked insulted.

"It's not like you to do fashion descriptions. You suck at it actually."

He wiped his brow with the back of a hand. "Thank God for small favors."

I chuckled. "Any other blips that night?"

"Yes and no. It's not a blip. It's serious. An attendee went out drinking with her friends after the event," he said. "They took a walk along the water at high tide and a wave swept her off the rocks. Witnesses say the waves were big that night, but that rogue wave came from nowhere."

"What happened to her?"

"Presumed drowned."

"Oh," I whispered, staring down at my gloves, my vision blurry.

Werner looked surprised. "Did you know her?"

"You didn't give me a name, so . . . no. It's just . . . sad. What about her friends? Are their names listed?"

He shook his head. "No, they were minors."

They were not minors. They were lying adults who probably thought after all these years that they'd gotten away with it. Except maybe . . . the man who stood watching my roof get raised?

"Wait," I said. "Presumed drowned?"

"Her body was never recovered. Her name was Robin O'Dowd. Seven years later, she was declared legally dead."

"By who?"

Eleven

Robin had died. She had not swum successfully to shore. I would not have wanted to read the morning papers the day after the country club's fiftieth.

I wanted answers to the questions the vision left me with, and if I couldn't get Werner to reopen the case, my only hope was that Deborah's gown would offer up a few clues. Or some of those old petticoat pieces would, wherever they happened to be forty years later—if they survived.

"Sarge?" Billings called after we heard a door open—it sounded like the kitchen.

Werner grunted. "Billings," he called. "We're in here." He waited for the officer to appear.

Billings tipped his nonexistent cap my way.

Werner had put everything back in my Vuitton case after he'd called Billings.

"Enter this in evidence—"

"Everything but my Vuitton case. You can return it to me when you're done with it, okay?"

"Yes, ma'am."

"Billings, we need to reopen the case file mentioned here." Werner handed Billings the printed page. "Find the original paperwork."

"I want the cash box and everything in it dusted for prints, even the scavenger-hunt list. Count the money, have it checked for forgery, try to find a match, prints, the works. See if you can get both cash box and snuffbox authenticated and valued. Were either of them, or any of the items on the scavenger list, reported missing in the past ninety or so years?" Werner slipped the list into a plastic zip bag, too. "Ditto on the two biggest bills. Try to find us a rare currency collector or expert to give us some history on these."

We watched Billings leave the house, heard him drive away.

Werner got up, came around his desk, and went to the closet for my jacket and purse. "Oh sorry, dropped your purse." He fumbled around. "Your stuff's probably mixed up inside it now."

I bit my tongue, and did not remind him how valuable Vuitton purses were.

Finally, he handed me my bag and held my jacket out for me to slip into. Message loud and clear: Go home, Madeira.

"I guess that's all the justice we can give it right now," he said. "Thanks for turning in the box, Mad."

"Glad to help," I said, the phrase "obstruction of justice" weighing me down like a funeral dirge in my limbs. Darn Chakra and her preoccupation with petticoat pieces.

I wondered if I could be charged for holding back the

piece the attic box had been wrapped in. I mean, if Werner interviewed Isaac, he'd know I received the box covered in fabric, then I'd be screwed, and not in a good way.

I nibbled my lip over losing that petticoat piece all the way home.

All the lights were on at Dad's, a nice change. He and Aunt Fiona were at our house and not hibernating.

I heard the screams and laughter before I opened the door. "Are you two babysitting?"

"What do you think?" my father asked as he was hit in the face with strained peas.

Babies Kathleen and Riley, my sister Sherry's five-month-old twins, were sitting in high chairs at the table, and it looked like Dad and Fee needed help.

Riley, our bouncing baby boy, aimed those peas with loud amusement, his laughter like a bubble of joy, especially when they hit my father's face. While Kathleen, our strawberry blonde charmer, ate hers with one pinky raised.

"They couldn't be more alike or more different, could they?" I asked.

Fiona shook her head. "No, they couldn't."

"Dad, do you always get Riley?"

"Yes." He sighed.

I wet a towel and came back to wash my father's face. Fee and I found that highly amusing, and the babies joined in our merriment. Before long, my grumpy father was laughing louder than all of us.

The scent of chocolate wafted through the room, and I knew that my mother saw her beautiful grandchildren and how happy Dad and Fee were.

"Mom approves," I said.

"I've come to accept your mom's signature scent, but it gets me every time. Happens mostly when the babies are here." He furrowed his brows. "Or you are."

When the babies finished eating, they, too, needed cleaning up. "I want to fix their curls," I said, and I went for the comb in my purse rather than run upstairs.

When I opened it, I squeaked. Inside I found the zip bag with the small piece of petticoat from around the diamond snuffbox. Werner hadn't dropped or fumbled my purse; he'd been shoving the evidence bag in there. Invisible, like it never happened. And I would return it the same way, first thing Monday morning, which meant that I should read it tonight.

I combed the babies' hair, played with them, and helped Fiona give them their baths, the two of us alone together for a bit. "Are they staying the night?" I asked.

"Yes, your sister needed a break."

"Obviously she didn't intend for Dad to keep them by himself."

"She's very cool about us being together," Aunt Fiona said. "Your dad appreciates that his family accepts us as a couple."

I chuckled. "Stubborn man."

Aunt Fee raised her brows. "Guess who takes after him?"

"Who, me?"

"I need to run something by you," she said, putting Riley back in his chair. "Sherry suggested that your nieces and nephews call me Nana—when they can talk, of course."

I hugged her. "That's wonderful. What was dad's reaction?"

"His eyes filled. I didn't know if he was happy for me or sad that your mother isn't here."

"Would a bit of both be so terrible?" I asked.

Fiona's frown lines relaxed. "I guess a bit of both would be normal."

"Face it, Fee, you are Nana to dad's Poppy, and he likes it that way. Look ahead, not back, and if you do look back now and again, try to focus on Mom throwing you kisses of approval, will you?"

Her eyes filled, and after another, longer, but silent hug, we each chose a rocker. I rocked my godson—mine and Nick's—while Fiona rocked Alex and Tricia's goddaughter.

After we put them down in the nursery Dad had set up, with cribs dating back to my day, we went downstairs, where Dad watched the History Channel.

"I have to say good night to the two of you," I said. "You'll probably be asleep by the time I get home."

"I didn't think you were going out again."

"I didn't think I was, either. But I realized there's an outfit I want to get a bead on."

"One bead?" My father asked. "You can sew a bead on tomorrow morning in, like, two seconds. Why go out again tonight?"

I kissed his brow. "To give you two some space," I said. "And really, I do have to spend some time on a particular piece."

I saw the knowledge register in Aunt Fiona's expression. "Get a bead on," she repeated. "I get it. You gonna be okay? Want company? The twins are down for the count. Your father can handle them."

"It's a bead, Fiona," my dad said, patting the space

beside him on the sofa. For a lit professor, he could be pretty literal. Of course he was distracted by Aunt Fiona; one look at her, and his metaphors morphed and popped like soap bubbles. Or he was being obtuse on purpose because he wanted me out of there.

I wanted to ask when he'd traded sitting strictly in that tweed chair, which bore the imprint of his body, for the sofa, but I knew better. "Have a good night, you two."

It got dark early now, I thought as I drove to the shop. I liked that I'd had motion-detector spotlights put up around the shop. No more dark parking lot all winter.

Thank goodness I also had an alarm system now, I thought, beeping myself in and then resetting it after I'd locked myself inside.

I hated walking into an empty shop. I had gotten used to having someone there to greet me, even a spectral someone. "Dante Underhill, I don't like it when you stay away. Are you hiding? I find that hard to believe. Like, what can I do if I'm upset with you, kill you?"

I put on some soft lighting in the sitting area, a couple of my mother's favorite lamps. "Anyway, I'm here to read a piece of fabric, so I might talk like a dead person or something, just so you don't get scared."

I chuckled. "Little tidbit for you to chew on: I miss you. I liked hearing you chuckle a couple times before. I knew that at least you were not upset with me."

I felt his feather touch on my cheek.

Then he was there, my Cary Grant clone in tux and top hat, looking into my eyes and caring that I missed him. "Thanks for not leaving that blasted music on every night, after all," he said.

"Despite your flamboyant past, you have integrity, so I figure there's a reason you're not talking."

"The name of the person who left the box doesn't matter to your case, Mad. I promise you. But it would matter to the quality of his life to be named. He was used. I need you to trust me on this."

Twelve

I love reading people. I really enjoy watching, observing, and being able to figure out a person, the reason they wore that dress, the reason they smell the way they do.

—RIHANNA

"I haven't even talked to you about the case, Dante," I said. "And you were dead when he showed up to hide it here, right?"

Dante nodded.

"So, how can you make that judgment?"

"We were kids together. He always got the short end; I can't even describe how. If I tell you who it is, it'll send you his way."

"But if he's not guilty, why would it matter?"

"He wouldn't hurt a fly. He cried as a kid over roadkill. He was used, I tell you."

"Who would have used him? They might be the guilty parties."

"The world was less enlightened then. People were not seen as being created equal. He was marked, and everybody had good aim. That's all I'm going to say on the matter. He might have been five when I passed, but I know that the publicity of being interviewed, singled out, would destroy him. I saw how scared he was when he left that box. He'd been threatened, and he believed the threats."

"You're sure, Dante, that he could be of no use to me?"

"None. I've heard you on the phone with Werner. Heard you with Eve. The piece of petticoat around the box and the peach gown are connected. I lived in this town. I belonged to the country club. I refused to take part in the scavenger hunts."

"They had them from the beginning, then?"

"They did."

"Anybody at the country club you don't feel any allegiance to?"

"Who aren't dead? Let me think about who was most likely to commit larceny. But, Mad, this is a lot of hullabaloo about a scavenger hunt and some missing baubles."

"Someone died the night that box was taken."

Dante's head came up. "Now that's a yardstick of a different shape. But you're smart. You don't need my help."

"I'll tell you what I do need."

"What's that?"

"Your friendship. I need you reading my paper when I come to work in the morning, your snarky comments when a woman squeezes into a dress two sizes too small. I miss our banter."

"I'm back, as long as we understand each other on this issue. And I won't hang you out to dry, Mad. If, in the end, knowing who left the box will solve the case, I'll tell you."

"Thanks, my friend."

"So what are you doing here so late?"

"I came to get another reading."

"Why didn't you bring Eve?"

"I'm afraid to give her a stroke."

"Let me sit with you while you read whatever you have, then."

I'm sure my doubt showed in my expression. "If I get into trouble, what could you do?"

"I could set off the alarm. That'd bring the police and an ambulance."

"Yes, it would. Thanks. I like knowing you're here." I took off my suit jacket, and, still wearing my gloves so as not to smudge any fingerprints on Werner's petticoat piece, I lay on my side on the fainting couch.

Dante sat beside me while I unzipped the evidence bag, turned it upside down and let the fabric, smaller than the piece wrapped around the box, waft down against my arm. "I got a reading only after the wind blew the first piece against my chin and cheeks outside," I said. "I can't get my prints on it, so I hope my bare arm will be enough for a psychometric connection."

"How do you feel?" Dante asked.

"Normal, and hoping I don't have to put it against my face. It's dirtier than the other." And there were brown spots on it. Blood? I shivered at the thought. I suspected that it had touched the floor of the whale belly as Vainglory took it off beneath her gown, which meant it hadn't been washed in at least forty years. Yuck.

Then I flew, without a broom, straight on until morning. I hadn't needed to put it against my face after all.

I found myself back in the belly of the whale, alone with a man, with the sun beginning to rise. I saw his back, the span of his shoulders, gauged his height. I watched him search as I hovered near the ceiling. My visions often happen this way. Sometimes I become a watcher without a body. Who knows why?

The lone searcher kept peeking into small places. He tucked something above a ceiling beam, walked around to look up there from every angle, swore, and took it down. He felt above the windows, the doors. Looked beneath the open stairs.

As the sun began to rise, what I had assumed was the belly of a boat—or maybe I wasn't even in the same place—turned into an empty brick mill or warehouse. The faded word "steam" was painted on the brick inside wall in capital letters about two feet high in Britannic Bold, or as near as, if I didn't miss my guess. Pieces of other words had been obliterated by replacement bricks. The rise and fall of the tide remained a constant if more distant sound. I surmised it to be low tide now, given the cleaner scent and the gentle wash of tides in the background. Certainly the storm had passed. Maybe by hours. Likely, this *was* the place they'd gathered after the scavenger hunt to determine who won the "game." I distinctly remembered not needing my sea legs, and this place did indeed smell of the briny sea.

I could see better now—a dilapidated warehouse, rubble on the floor, like a couple of broken old chairs, one overturned, an old rubber tire with a cat curled inside, an ancient filthy sink in the corner. Likely the same gathering place, the loner's tux suggested it could be the same night, or perhaps he'd been to a wedding. One indisputable fact: time was definitely toward morning.

For certain, the others were gone; they'd left the jubilee that had taken place the night before.

Tuxman paced and swore. "Just one small hiding place?" he begged loudly toward the rafters in a voice I did not recognize from my previous visions. His cry echoed and bounced as if pummeling him with the mayhem of the night.

He punched a column, bent over and swore at himself, and examined his bloody knuckles. Proof of self-recrimination, to my mind.

He touched the same column, felt along the joint he'd smacked, turned toward the center of the rancid depot, and shouted as if his favorite team had scored.

He fetched a wooden toolbox, or carrier, from a closet with a door split vertically down the middle. He moved like he knew this place. He then made for the center stairs.

As he climbed, he cackled—no other way to describe the self-satisfied sound—as he caressed slapdash handrails made of fat, jointed pipes, maybe three inches in diameter. The construction of the railings reminded me of anything made with Tinkertoys. Or metal plumber's pipe.

In some cases, two pieces made one upright or two formed one span from upright to upright. Likely built during the Depression, they were a good indication of the way people made do with whatever they could get their hands on. In our neck of the woods, you never discounted anything built in this piece-by-piece way as having arrived in parts, over time, from the subbase.

Tuxman looked nefarious, working in tails on a T joint halfway up a dirty, worn, raw-wood stairway. He'd chosen a spot where two pieces of handrail met an upright. He cursed plenty until the T finally gave and fell, *clunk, clunk,*

clunk down the stairs then with a pipe-meets-cement clang onto a dust-caked, greasy floor.

Another string of curses ensued as he failed to access the inside of the pipe. The two handrail pieces met atop the upright, blocking his access.

I saw his dilemma.

"The idiots who built this should be shot!" he snapped.

I really did not recognize Tuxman's voice.

A distant whistle scared the fiberfill out of us both. Tuxman jumped like he'd nearly had a heart attack, which caused him to fall halfway down the stairs. One leg caught around a rail and his head hit the floor. Then a *whoosh* shook the rafters and grime rained down on him, as he lay there in openmouthed shock.

I'll confess to a spark of amusement as he spit and coughed and swore, and then pulled himself up and together and got back to work.

What shook the building had been a train that had rushed by, of course. First of the morning would be my guess. The mill must sit alongside the tracks, as most of Mystic's old mills did. Once upon a time, the railroad would have been their prime shippers.

Tuxman wiped his face, pulled on his tails, got all dignified again, and hung on the upright like a monkey. With his whole body, he pulled the top toward him while pushing against the bottom, and when it moved the slightest bit forward, he took something from his pocket, a small item that looked to be wrapped in a petticoat piece, and slipped it into the pipe. Then he added two more objects, both wrapped, to the hollow pipe, one longer and narrower than the others.

With a relieved sigh, he pushed it back into place, and resecured the T joint with the tools. Good as new, except he'd tarnished the natural grungy patina on the old silver pipes. So he went from upright to handrail, tarnishing pipes all the way up to the third floor. Neatness did not count. I assume he wanted to make them all look equally distressed.

A single round of applause echoed in the empty place, another mocking sound.

Tuxman and I whipped our gazes toward the intruder.

"You scared me," Tuxman said. "I thought you went home with your brother."

"Nah. I'm not scared," a new voice said. He stood on the verge of adulthood but looked to be stuck there. His voice hadn't yet changed, and he gave the impression of insecurity, like a tagalong unsure of his welcome, acting younger than his size and voice implied. Too young to be part of a murder.

"Nothing scares you," Tuxman said, patronizing the lanky boy. "Did you hide yours yet?"

"Nah. Saw you hide yours, though. I might hide mine with Day's toy cars."

Tuxman slapped the kid on the back. "I'm not sure that a hiding place as close as Bradenton Cove is a good idea. You'd be better off to hide it on the Yachtsee."

"I scavenged more junk than you. But I don't got stair pipes to hide it in. I could stuff 'em down a drainpipe?"

"A heavy rain'll wash 'em to the ground."

"Oh." The intruder's shoulders went up, then fell in a dejected manner. "I would have won the scavenger hunt, if not for—" Quick switch of emotion, like a younger child, off to the next subject.

Tuxman clamped a bony hand on the young shoulder and squeezed visibly.

"Ouch."

"Sorry. Listen, kid, you did win. But you can never, ever tell."

"Ohh-kay! Kin we play again tomorrow?"

Play? Like an innocent. Dante's words came back to me. Someone who had been used.

What a misinterpretation of that night's events.

Thirteen

"Am I not brilliant?" I asked.

Eve made a show of huffing and turning to face me from the passenger seat of her black Mini Cooper, since sleuthing made her too nervous to drive. And my Element was too big, boxy—and purple—to be inconspicuous.

"Madeira, you heard, in a psychometric stupor, a childlike scavenger say he'd hide something at Bradenton Cove. So forty years later you find the place and we, like idiots, head out to an estate that may, or may not, be the same Bradenton Cove?"

I knew for certain that it was one and the same. When I woke from my psychometric vision, I told Dante about it. He said the famous Bradenton Cove in Watch Hill, Rhode Island, known for their vintage car collection, was situated just the other side of Stonington and Mystic.

A founding country club family had owned the estate

for generations. Dante gave no names. I asked for none. He'd played there as a boy and suggested removing the fifth chimney brick from the bottom left at the back of the garage for a key that should be used on the cellar door at the bottom of a dug-out stairway as a quiet means of entering the area where they kept the classic cars. But I couldn't tell Eve that. She didn't know that Dante existed. And she didn't want to.

I dressed to sleuth in a Kamali jumpsuit, python bomber jacket, and a funky pair of Converse sneakers, the easier to climb around and run in, if necessary.

Of course the family, the cars, the garage—they might all be gone by now. But I had to try. For Robin. "You said you wanted to live dangerously," I pointed out.

"So I did," Eve admitted. "Which makes us both crazy, but it makes neither of us brilliant."

"This is wildly exciting. Admit it," I prompted her.

"I'll let you know after I throw up," she grumbled.

"Hah! Glad we're in your car."

"What does this place look like?" she asked after a quiet few minutes.

I gave her the map. "I Googled it, got an aerial view. We'll drive down the hill on the right, park behind the huge waterfront garage, depart via the hill on the left, and in between we'll see what we can find."

"Trouble. We're gonna find trouble."

"Day's cars," she said. "Didn't you say he was gonna hide the stuff with Day's cars? That's nuts."

Dante had told me that Day meant dad in that family, which helped. I just had to look in the garage. It sounded so easy. Too easy.

When we arrived, the house looked totally dark. So I turned off the car lights and coasted down the drive and around back behind the extra-wide quad garage.

It was nearly as big as my shop; probably a carriage house at one time as well.

Peeking in the window on the bottom level revealed some amazing vintage cars. "We're in the right place. Go peek around the side to see if there are any lights in the house on this side," I asked.

Eve did, while I fetched the key.

When she returned, I was standing in the open basement door at the bottom of a set of cement stairs. "It was open," I said. "Any lights?"

"No. What is it, opera night?"

"Friday is buffet night at the country club. If we're lucky, they go to a movie after."

"Hey, whaddaya know?"

I knew nothing. "That the basement is pristine and the stairs to the garage are dark," I whispered.

They squeaked and groaned something horrific.

"Heart attack stairs," Eve said.

"Tell me about it."

It took some hunting and walking around quite the collection of vintage cars to find a piece of pipe, because I believed that the young man was a follower. He'd wanted to hide it in a pipe, in this garage.

I prayed that he'd stuck to his plans despite the warning of his older friend to find a better hiding place than the garage.

In the work area—where no cars were parked, except a turquoise Corvette that seemed to need bodywork—tools reigned supreme. We found an extra-deep shelf—like maybe fifteen, twenty feet deep—built up near the ceiling, for items like lengths of wood, floorboards, shelving, two-by-fours, drainpipes, studs, drywall; that kind of thing. And in the midst of them, I saw the edge of the stored ladder.

"Fat lot of good that'll do," Eve whispered, eyeing the ladder.

I found a power lift, but no key. We were forced to build a tower out of crates, trunks, toolboxes, anything square and at least semi-sturdy, and we set them up in a way that they could be climbed, like stairs, to get to the shelf.

By the time I got to maybe the fourth step, and the drainpipe still looked as far up as the top of the Mystic Bridge open for shipping traffic, the whole stack wobbled, and I yipped.

"Down, Mad," Eve ordered. "Right this minute."

"But I have to get the—"

"I'm the tomboy, remember? I saved your ascot when you jumped ship, remember?"

"Well, that's a matter of—"

"Get down, brat. You shine designing clothes. Me, I climb like a monkey."

"You'd be dressing like one, too, if it weren't for me."

"I know. To thank me, can you get down, please?"

Climbing down was scarier than going up.

"You're right," I said, watching Eve. "You climb like a monkey."

Making monkey noises, she kept going.

The piece of drainpipe I asked her to pull out measured about three feet. She aimed it toward me and looked through it like a telescope. "Bad news, Mad. I can see you. There's nothing in it."

I gave a hard, involuntary shiver and turned more hot than cold. "It's got to be there."

"Wait," Eve said. "I see a small piece that I can almost reach. Oh, wait, I'll knock it closer with this piece of molding." As she did, she made a few banging noises.

"Eve, shush."

"You shush. I'm doing the best I can."

"They'll hear us."

"They're at the country club. And we're a mile from the mansion."

I heard a *pop*, and a piece of drainpipe came flying from the shelf. It bounced twice off our tower, knocking two of the upper pieces off the pile. I jumped out of the way, but the drainpipe's trajectory had been changed, and it bounced off the hood of the Corvette.

Two things happened at once.

An ear-splitting alarm went off, and Eve monkeyed her way deeper into the overhang. So much for running away.

I climbed up the toppling tower, grabbed Eve's hand, and scraped my side as she pulled me into the overhang. She shoved our tower with a two-by-four so the pieces scattered to the far side of the repair shop.

The two of us scrambled as deep into the overhang as we could go, and huddled silent as mice, me praying that it would hold our weight.

The garage lit up like a Christmas tree.

Fourteen

Why not be one's self? That is the whole secret of a success-ful appearance. If one is a greyhound, why try to look like a Pekingese?   —EDITH SITWELL, 1887–1964

For the longest time, the only sound I could hear was my own heart beating in my head. My gut ached from tension and my eyes were screwed so tightly shut, I gave myself a headache.

When I unclenched, my eyes opened. Nothing had actually happened. We'd tripped something, but with nobody at the house, who knew?

With the light on, I looked around and found, right next to me, the oddest thing. A piece of drainpipe, about a foot long, but capped at each end. I shook it a bit and something inside slid. When I went to put it in my purse, I realized I'd left that on the floor.

I was shaken by the adventure and stupidly worried that somebody would take my Coach tote.

Eve grabbed my hand and pointed. Car lights moved down the hill toward us.

Eve scrambled forward, sat at the edge, jumped from there, and landed on the roof of the Corvette.

I followed her. This was going to cost us.

Eve went for the door. "Let's get your freaky ass out of here."

I didn't take the time to check the capped pipe. I stuffed it into my bag, and we went out the door closest to our car. The building alarm went off as we got in the car and I peeled out from behind the garage.

People stepped from a Beemer as we passed.

"They saw us!" Eve whispered. "Drive faster," she said. "One of them was nine-one-oneing on a cell phone."

"The cops?" I asked.

"How the hell do I know who they'd call when their million-dollar car collection gets invaded, unless they stole the cars."

I slowed down to take a left onto the highway.

Eve gasped. "South on 95? Are you nuts? Back roads, you twit," she ordered.

That made sense, except that I then took a road I didn't know.

"I can't go as fast on a back road," I pointed out as I slowed down.

"That's okay, we'll be harder to find if the police come after us."

"If? Look behind us," I suggested. "Is it my imagination, or do the spaces between the trees in the woods behind us look kind of red and blue?"

Eve squeaked. "Drive faster."

I took a quick left, and we found ourselves in an upper-class development of Victorian houses. "There must have been a black-and-white in the vicinity to get here so fast," I said.

"Ya think? Duh. The flash between the trees is keeping up," she said.

That's when I realized I'd driven into a circle. The garage attached to the house at the center was open and empty. I turned off my lights, headed for that driveway, and into the garage.

Eve began hyperventilating. "What are you doing, Looney Tune?"

"Hiding in plain sight?"

"That's what you think."

"Shut up," I said.

"Shut up and duck," Eve amended. "Werner wouldn't approve of what we did tonight. Nick either," she added.

"They're probably the only ones who would understand, though," I said beneath my breath, our heads near the gearshift.

I peeked behind us. Scrap, scrap, scrap. A police car, not the state police, but a local Rhode Island cop, drove into the circle.

I held my breath again. Funny how I always closed my eyes when I did that.

"Oh my gosh, they're leaving," Eve said. "We can go now."

I put the car in gear . . . and slammed on the brakes.

The garage lights came on and we got spot-lit from behind.

"Is it the cop?" Eve asked.

"You wish," I said.

Whoever it was blocked our exit, got out of the car, and came toward the driver's side. My side.

"Act drunk," I whispered, before I rolled down my window.

An older woman bent down to look in at us. A nurse, probably home from the late shift at a hospital. "And you're sitting in my garage because . . . ?"

"Mom?" I asked, pretending to be muddled, yes, but actually calling for help from my mom.

"Are you drunk?" the nurse asked.

"Tired maybe," I said. "I'm the designated driver."

"Honest, Mrs. . . . Mom," Eve said. You should be lelling at me. Yelling. That's the word."

"I am not your mother, young lady, for which I give thanks."

Wow, I thought, the light must be really bad in here, if she thinks we're young ladies.

"But the house is the right color," I said. "Last one in the circle, driveway on a hill." I turned to Eve. "Did we take a wrong turn?"

"Get out of the car," the nurse said, closing her long, heavy gray sweater coat. "Where do you live?"

"Mystick Falls," I said, turning off the car and sliding from my seat.

"Are you gonna keep us for ransom?" Eve asked, as she fake tripped getting out.

"I'm taking you home. Which set of parents gets you both, or are you sisters?"

"Friends," I said. "But what about my car?"

"Best ever friends," Eve added, playing her role well.

"You can come back for your car tomorrow afternoon."

"But where are we?"

"I'll write down my address after I hand you over to your parents." Our captor indicated that I should get in her front passenger seat and she put Eve in the back. She even buckled Eve's seatbelt.

"Why don't you just let us go?" I asked before we left. "I mean, if you're this kind?"

"Because one or both of you have been drinking, and I'm a nurse. I know what can go wrong. I've seen it too many times to have the possibility on my conscience."

"You're a good person."

"When I hand you to your family you won't think so. Who am I taking you to?"

"My brother," I said, and I gave her Werner's address.

Eve yipped.

The nurse looked in the rearview mirror. "Hiccups. Typical. Just don't get carsick. I just had this detailed."

When she left the circle, she had to wait to take a right until a police car went by, and Eve hiccupped again.

"See that policeman?" the woman said. "He could have stopped you and been hauling your drunk behinds to the police station right now. You lucked out driving into my garage."

"You don't even know us," I said.

"It occurred to me that you could have been planning to rob my house, but I'm a pretty good judge of character. I see no harm in you. I think your friend's a bit of a loose cannon, but you have the air of a helper about you."

"Like Santa's helper?" I asked, and Eve giggled.

"Someone who helps people, like nurses do. I'm guessing you try to help and sometimes you get into trouble for it."

First, I wanted to hug her. It was like I had gotten my mom after all. Then I wanted to tell her that maybe we were both psychic, but she hadn't caught that we were in trouble or that Eve was faking. On the other hand, maybe she did know.

"I'm Addy," she said. "You?"

There were witnesses who'd seen us leave Bradenton Cove. "I'm Mad-eline, and that's my friend Ev-e-lyn. You can call us Mad and Eve. Eve's a genius, by the way. She just has a weird sense of style."

"It takes all kinds."

"I'd like to thank you for being the kind to rescue a coupl'a girls who took a wrong turn and ended up invading your home."

"You'll pay it forward, I think."

"Count on it."

All too soon, we were pulling up in front of Werner's . . . at nearly three in the morning. I sure hoped he'd play at being my brother.

Addy, our rescuer, leaned on the doorbell nonstop.

A grouchy Werner whipped open the door, looking ready to bark or aim a gun at us, cantankerous but yummy in a navy brocade robe with tousled hair and big bare feet.

"Mad, what the heck?"

I threw my arms around him. "You're such an understanding brother. Try now, pleeeze."

Fifteen

One wants to be very something, very great, very heroic; or if not that, then at least very stylish and very fashionable.

—HARRIET BEECHER STOWE

I stepped back. "Addy, this is my brother, Lytton. Bro, this is Addy. We sort of got lost and drove into her garage by mistake."

Yeah, he'd buy that.

Addy's head came up, and she leaned back to look at the house, then toward Lytton's driveway. "You know, this house looks nothing like mine. It's not even in a cul de sac."

"No, but our mother's is," I said, and when Werner opened his mouth, I sort of stepped on his bare little toe, easy like.

Werner rocked on his heels, mostly to get away from my brutality, and he gave the woman a half nod. I was so in for it with him.

Addy poked the top of my arm. "This one drove into my garage by mistake—drunk, the both of them. That one," she said, aiming her thumb toward Eve behind her, "so much the worse for it." Addy was a tall woman, broad shouldered and strong, with a kind face and a big, caring heart.

"With the drink, I couldn't let them drive. You can bring one of them back to my house tomorrow between noon and three, if that's all right? Is that your car in the drive?" She nodded toward the police car.

"My car's in the shop," Werner said, "so I borrowed a squad car for the weekend."

"He runs the place," I told her.

"Well, then I'm leaving you in good hands. Don't let these two drink and drive again, if you please. I don't want the next time I meet them to be in Lawrence Memorial Hospital."

Eve hiccupped for good measure.

Werner put his hand on my shoulder. Hard. "Sure thing," he said. "Mad will reimburse you for your gas when she picks up her car tomorrow, right, sis?" he asked, his fingers digging into my shoulder.

I ducked from beneath his grasp. "Of course, bro."

We stood in the doorway and waved Addy off. I was thinking of something nice from my shop that I could bring her, along with the gas reimbursement. "Thanks for the rescue," I called, before she got into her Honda Insight, then we watched her drive away.

Werner shut his door. "Okay, give."

Of course, Werner couldn't know about our personal scavenger hunt for petticoat pieces to read for clues and how I'd known where to find them, so I prevaricated a wee bit. "I got a phone call at the shop. A tip from an anonymous source, maybe somebody who saw Isaac find the box and knew what it was. I don't know. But he"—meaning Dante—"told me where to find the key to the garage and that I'd find some of the scavenger hunt 'loot' in an old piece of drainpipe."

And from that fabricated beginning, Eve and I took turns telling Werner the truth, every detail, from then on.

"Breaking and entering, Madeira?"

"With a key someone gave me the location of."

He grumped. "So, what did you find?"

"Oh," I said. "I didn't look in the drainpipe." I opened my bag and took out the double-capped, foot-long piece, but I couldn't pry off either cap.

"I'll get it," Werner said, taking it into his garage.

Eve and I curled up on separate ends of Werner's sofa to wait.

He had to wake us when he came back with an open piece of drainpipe.

"What's in it?" I asked

"Like with the cash box, I waited to open it with you." He set a newspaper on the coffee table. "I'll shake it out gently, shall I? And we can't touch, because we're not wearing gloves."

First item to slide out: a plastic toy soldier.

"Son of a stitch, he didn't hide it in a drainpipe after all. He was slow. A boy in a man's body."

Werner's brows furrowed. "What did you say?"

"A boy in a man's body. He was gonna hide his treasure in a drainpipe with his father's vintage cars."

"You met him?"

"No, he was . . . talkative."

"Like a man who acted like a boy? Tells too much?"

"You got it." Scrap, I needed to learn to shut up and sort out my visions from my reality . . . and from my lies. Lies for the greater good, I told myself. Funny how I couldn't buy that one.

"Maybe this is his idea of a treasure," Werner said. "Just not what you were sleuthing for."

"I'm bummed." I huffed.

"You're not gonna hit it every time, but we're not done." Werner shook the drainpipe again. Another soldier fell out, as well as some kind of antique decoder ring that hadn't been listed on the scavenger-hunt list.

"These are just random toys, not from the scavenger-hunt list. Treasures to a little boy, that's all."

"Right. You lucked out," Werner said. "We couldn't have entered stolen goods into evidence, anyway. Don't try that again."

I leaned against his shoulder because I was feeling tired and grateful. "I feel pretty stupid. Thanks for being so understanding."

He rubbed my back for a minute, put a half a moment's pressure against it—a wish of a hug, really—and let me go. I pulled away and sat straighter, but the imprint of his touch lingered. Caring, likely not planning his next promotion.

Werner capped the drainpipe and put it and the toys back in my purse, effectively breaking the moment between us.

"Now what?" I asked.

"Wake up Gothzilla," he said, turning out the lights and making a motion for us to precede him up the stairs. "The whole Mystick Falls force knows your license plate, Mad. If Rhode Island decides to run it, you're toast."

"If they got the plate," I said. "But, we took Eve's car. So we may not need to cross that bridge." I shook Eve, got her standing, and followed Werner. Eve walked into me in the middle of the upstairs hallway when I stopped short. "Where are we going?"

"I'm not driving you home now. What do you want to sleep in, a T-shirt or a button-down?" And then he deadpanned. "My bed or yours?"

"You'd sleep on the sofa for us?" I touched my hand to my heart.

Werner firmed his lips and sighed.

Eve hiccupped a giggle. She really did sound drunk.

I shrugged. "Eve will take the tee, and I prefer a button-down."

He took us into his room. "Third drawer, Eve. Take your pick. Button-downs in the closet, Mad. Bottom drawer if you want bottoms. Sweatpants in there. Does Nick know what kind of trouble you get into when he's away?"

"He didn't have time to listen, said you'd be here for me if I needed you, and you are." I threw my arms around him for a brotherly hug. "Thanks."

He held on until I stepped from his arms and left with a purple-striped button-down on my way to the guest bathroom.

"New toothbrushes in the right-hand drawer," our host called.

"'Kay, thanks."

I stuck my head out the door. "Eve, are you teaching tomorrow?"

"It's Saturday, but some of my computer students are competing in the International Collegiate Cyber Shield Competition. It has to do with protecting an ultra classified network infrastructure, and I'm their coach, so the short answer—too late—is 'Yes, I am.'"

"Werner, can you take me to pick up Eve's car around noon?"

"Sure."

"How am I getting to the Avery Point campus, then?" Eve asked.

"You can take my Element."

"Werner, can you bring me to Mad's Element around nine tomorrow?"

"He can do that after he brings me to my shop for eight thirty, can't you, Werner?"

"Sure, sis. Night, you drunken brats."

Sixteen

Clothes can suggest, persuade, connote, insinuate, or indeed lie, and apply subtle pressure while speaking frankly and straightforwardly of other matters. —ANNE HOLLANDER

Saturday, I needed to play the pre-holiday—Valentine's Day—sale game I'd advertised, so no time to think about the case, my stupid sleuthing trip to Bradenton Cove, or the formals I'd have to judge.

Dolly and Aunt Fee took the lunch crowd—usually much thinner—while Werner took me to pick up Eve's car at Addy's house.

"Mind if we do a drive-by of your crime scene?" Werner asked.

I shivered. "Must we?" I caught the whine in my voice as I shrank down into my seat while a wash of heat rose up my neck to fire my cheeks. I rolled down the passenger-side window. "Such a fiasco."

"Trust me, you lucked out. Nobody's looking for you. I know. I checked first thing this morning."

"You could've called and told me. Set my mind at ease."

"No, I thought you should stew for a while. No more straddling the knife-sharp edge of felonious sleuthing, Mad. Seriously. My protection extends only so far."

"I hear you. You don't have to yell."

"I didn't yell."

"Your voice rose with every word."

"Sorry. There are some things—and people—I get passionate about."

What could I say to that? "You get passionate about me?" Okay, I was asking for it. There was something totally me, the essence of Madeira Cutler, that I liked about myself when I was with Werner. No show. No stand-by-your-Fed facade.

He gave me a double take and drove slowly, silently along the main road that fronted Bradenton Cove, so easily visible from up here. The shape of the driveway reminded me of an old-fashioned lock design, with the house and garage beyond it sitting in the circle at the top lock's giant inverted U.

Along the road, a man of mature years out for a stroll, handsome and gray at the temples, hailed us with his cane.

"Scrap, scrap, scrap!" I scooted down a bit more in the seat. And then I decided I wasn't made to be invisible. So I sat up and raised my chin.

"Good girl," Werner said as he slowed and rolled down his window for the guy who'd come right up to it, like he wanted to chat. "There's a flask hidden in my cane," he said, with the man's voice of the little tagalong boy who'd found someone hiding scavenger-hunt treasures in the stair-rail pipe of an old warehouse. "I keep lemonade in it. Day won't let me have brandy."

Day. Yep, same boy. Maybe the one coerced into hiding

the box in my attic. "Were you friends with Dante Underhill when you were a kid?"

The man's eyes filled. "He was my best friend. Died, ya know."

"I know. I'm sorry."

"Wanna see my flask?"

I whipped my gaze to Werner. He knew the item had been on the scavenger list.

"Sure," Werner said, looking appropriately interested. "Heard you had a break-in?"

The man nodded. "Thanks for watching, but nothin's missing. Not even a real break-in. My Day says just a nosy intruder. He's changin' the locks. My brother, though, he was some big mad."

"Who's your brother?" I asked.

"Eric . . . McDowell. I'm Zavier." He offered his hand to Werner, who shook it, then he came around to shake mine. "I still live here; I always lived here. Eric don't."

Zavier—also known to me as Tagalong, the unacknowledged brother of Councilman Eric McDowell—aka Grody. McDowell, a politician who'd break his arm patting himself on the back, had made my skin crawl from day one. That's why he'd seemed familiar in my visions. I knew him in the present. I hadn't placed him initially. In that first vision, he'd been so much younger—and scared. He'd legitimately seemed scared to death that Robin couldn't swim.

When I thought about it now, his crumpled, grungy tux with the stench of drying-seawater-soaked wool—that could put him square at the murder scene. If there had been a murder.

Zavier, well, he was well over fifty years old now, but he

didn't see the difference between our Connecticut black-and-white and a Rhode Island cruiser. And he still called his father Day. Not Dad.

"So, no damage?" Werner asked him.

"Only the car," Zavier said. "Day says somebody with a grudge against Corvettes took a sledge hammer to it."

Werner gave me a quick, questioning glance.

I rolled my eyes at the exaggeration.

I heard a man in the distance calling to Zavier. "You'd better go in," I said. So whoever was coming up the hill wouldn't see us.

"Yes, ma'am. Come again."

"Not on your life." I rolled up my window. "Drive."

Werner drove slowly away. "I get it now. A boy in a man's body. No way he knew what he was doing back then. Besides, one of the scavenger-hunt items forty years later is hardly proof."

"The cane and flask, yeah. He only took part in the scavenger hunt because his brother did. I just failed to find his stash. But you're right, he didn't know he was breaking the law, or that someone died that night."

I hadn't seen Zavier in the first vision, unless he'd stood back silently watching, the way he'd watched Tuxman toward dawn in the later vision.

I'd been so lost in my thoughts, I didn't notice for a few moments that Werner had pulled up the drive to Addy's house. "So you drove right into that garage?"

"With a cop on my tail, yeah."

"Just when I convince myself that you're nothing special, you do something to raise yourself in my esteem, you ballsy woman."

"My being ballsy doesn't emasculate you."

He roared.

"Don't make fun of me."

"You have the opposite effect, and you know it."

"I use my eyelashes to good effect."

"Sure, come on to me at the house of a nice lady who thinks I'm your brother. You know, you could have found a psychopath living here instead of a new millennium Clara Barton."

"Okay, that's enough." I took out the Vintage Magic shopping bag I'd brought and went to the front door.

Addy looked happy and shocked to see me. "You knew I'd come for the car," I said.

"I didn't know you'd be dressed like a million bucks," she responded. "I had you pegged different."

I guessed that my Gilbert Adrian black wool suit with purple trim and Todd Oldham purple-and-yellow spectator pumps kind of threw her. I looked down at myself. "I'm having a sale at my vintage dress shop today. Just took time off to pick up the car."

I slipped the shopping bag into her hand. "I put a check for the gas inside with my business card, and I picked out a Fendi purse and a Ferragamo wool cape from my shop to say thanks. I hope you like them."

"You didn't need to—"

"I know. And neither did you. Stop at my shop someday, and I'll take you to lunch."

She remained slack-jawed on her stoop, my bag hanging from her hand, as she watched me back Eve's car from her garage. I waved, and so did Addy, as I drove away, Werner right behind me.

He beeped as I turned onto Bank Street and headed home. Poor man was having a helluva day off.

The two-day sale exhausted me, but my mind stayed sharp. By Sunday night, I had concluded three things.

One: Eve and I had to try to find that mill or warehouse near the railroad tracks by the ocean. I already had an idea where to look.

Two: At least two of the scavengers had chosen abandoned buildings, my house and that mill, to hide their stolen property in. I'd ask Dolly and a couple of other circumspect seniors what buildings had been abandoned about forty years ago.

Three: I'd give Werner the pieces of fabric I'd read, though I wouldn't call them petticoat pieces, of course. I'd bring them to him when I met him at the country club first thing tomorrow. Now that I had the psychometric visions they inspired, my personal set of clues, we could find out what forensics had to say about them. Of course, one would have butterscotch cat hairs on it. Chakra had found her way into the last horse-drawn hearse upstairs and had used the fabric to make something of a nest, along with other pieces of scrap fabric she'd snitched from beneath my sewing machines.

Werner was expecting the second piece. He might not notice right away that I was giving him two.

Especially since he hadn't asked me to join him at the country club. Nor did I hint that I'd be there. I'd surprise him and give him the fabric my box had been wrapped in, which might make him more agreeable to my presence.

With my luck, he'd smell a rat. Or a cat.

Seventeen

For the country club: The goal is to create a polished outfit
that's a cut above your favorite casual look.
—HILLARY KERR AND KATHERINE POWER,
WHAT TO WEAR, WHERE

I could meet Werner at the country club and open the shop
later.

Oh no, I couldn't. More Golden Jubilee costumes, from
which I would choose the *This Is Your Life*rs, were being
delivered first thing tomorrow. But really, did I need to be
at the shop to accept a delivery?

I called Eve's mother and asked her to open the shop in
the morning. Mrs. Meyers seemed delighted and insisted on
calling her own helpers, her choices being equal to mine.
She'd get Dolly Sweet, who'd practically given me the building for my shop, and Dolly's no-nonsense daughter-in-law,
Ethel, less sprightly at 80 than Dolly at, 106.

Nevertheless, Ethel was a hard worker. She always
OCD'd the place into neat perfection and annihilated
every dust mote. Mrs. Meyers curled the customers around
her little finger with her soft German accent and sweet

personality. Dolly always made fun of them both before she disappeared into the farthest nook, the one called Paris when it Sizzles.

There, she and Dante rekindled a flame that defied the laws of physics.

I could sum up these special helpers into precise individual pet names: Neaty, Sweety, and Sparky.

In my absence, nobody could run the shop better, and they were all loved by my designer-vintage clientele.

I always hesitated to ask the ladies to work, because they wouldn't take a wage. However, they knew that if they were keen on an item, I'd let them walk away with it, providing the purse, shoes, dress, whatever hadn't been designed by Paul Poirot, or worn in Hollywood back in the day by Liz Taylor, Princess Grace, Vivien Leigh, or one of the Hepburns. You get my drift.

That kind of value vintage ran into the thousands, and the ladies knew it. You could usually only find those in a museum exhibit or on a state-of-the-art mannequin encased in bulletproof glass with an alarm system. But sometimes, rarely, I got lucky and found one for the shop.

Since this work trade-off had become something of a ritual during one of my sleuthing phases, my workers chose their payments fairly, and I always knew what else they liked, and therefore what to get them for holiday gifts.

I picked up coffee and doughnuts and then the ladies themselves around eight thirty the next morning. Mrs. Meyers and I let Dolly and Ethel entertain us by sniping at each other on the drive to the shop.

When we opened, they all looked to me for instructions.

"What?" I asked. "You know what to do."

"No special displays to take down, put up?" Mrs. Meyers asked. "Nothing new to fold?"

"We can always refold the items her customers messed up." Ethel sniffed in disdain for non-folders everywhere. "No special events to prep for, like upcoming holiday sales?"

"Oh, only one thing," I said, so entertained, I'd nearly forgotten. "A shipment will be delivered this morning of pricey costumes that were worn to the country club's fiftieth anniversary dinner dance in 1973. Leave them in their garment bags and hang them on the empty racks I've left behind the counter wall. If you don't have enough racks, there are more behind Paris when it Sizzles. Just don't open the bags. What's in them doesn't belong to me and isn't for sale."

They nodded and proceeded like guards to their posts, all except Dolly. She walked the wide display aisle that separated the front-wall nooks from those on the back wall, took a sharp right, and disappeared. "I'll clean Paris," she called behind her.

Yeah, right.

"Clean Paris?" Ethel scoffed. "That one gave up cleaning when she turned a hundred."

Very few people, besides me and Aunt Fiona, knew the building was haunted, much less by Dolly's scandalous lover. I've never even told Eve. She gets freaked when I read a piece of vintage clothing, because I sometimes speak in the voice of the person I occupy, unless I find myself floating somewhere nearby, watching. At any rate, Eve couldn't take the knowledge of Dante; she'd run screaming from the shop and never return if she knew.

"It's Dolly's favorite nook," I said. "Let her enjoy her twilight years."

"She's been enjoying them for two decades," Ethel observed. "You'd think she'd like Little Black Dress Lane once in a while. She could chose what she'd like to be buried in."

I bit my lip so as not to appear amused. "Her heart's in Paris, don't forget." And I meant that two ways.

Ethel snapped a finger. "That's right. Her brother went 'home' to Paris to live out his twilight years, and he took his granddaughter, Paisley, with him. Dolly was pretty bummed about that for a couple of months, but she's planning to visit them in the spring."

"That's Dolly, always putting a positive spin on things and planning for the future." I waved and left the shop.

Werner was getting out of his unmarked car when I got to the country club. "What do you think you're doing here?" he asked.

"Sleuthing? I can help. I'm getting good at this."

"No, you can't. You can't officially investigate a crime."

"Why not? Castle does it all the time."

"That's fiction, Mad. This is real life."

"Open your briefcase," I ordered.

He did, and I took the two evidence bags from my Bonnie Cashin blue purse, and slipped them into his briefcase. "Now shut it."

"There are two."

"You weren't supposed to mention it. This never happened."

"Where did the extra one come from?"

"It was wrapped around the brass money box in my attic."

"Why didn't you give it to me with the box?"

"Chakra fell in love with it, and when I wasn't looking, she stole it. I was still looking for it when I brought you the box. I wanted to see if she'd do the same with the second one. I used it for bait, and it worked. Thanks, by the way."

"What I did never happened," he said. "What you did—"

"Should never again be mentioned. Mistakes have been made; they will never be repeated."

His expression became searching, like . . . he was trying to search my thoughts, sure I must be hiding something.

"Sheesh," I said. "You look like you don't trust me."

He shook his head. "There are times I think you know more than any of us. And though I like working with you—which you will never repeat—I don't know how I can account for having you with me."

"We don't even know if it was a crime," I said, knowing better, deep inside. "Tell the country club people that the cash box was found on my property. Finders keepers, you know. If no one makes a claim on the cash box, I get to keep it, right? There's a record of one being lost at the silver anniversary, but was one also lost at the Golden Jubilee? We need answers, right? Both of us."

"Flimsy, flimsy, flimsy," Werner said.

"Okay, introduce me as the friend who's judging outfits for the *This Is Your Life* segment of their upcoming event, the Very Vintage Valentine ball. I'm working with the chairpersons for the event. I need to see the banquet facilities and ballroom, so we're killing two birds, and all that."

"Well, that's a bit sturdier than flimsy," he said on a sigh.

I curled my arm around his and squeezed. "Thanks, partner."

"Detective," he said, removing my arm. "You'll call me Detective, Ms. Cutler, or get back into your car."

I saluted.

The banquet manager greeted us and led us to her office. She offered us coffee and even breakfast pastries and settled down to answer our questions, until they got dicey. Werner started small and ticked off his queries on his fingers. "We need a list of attendees who came to the silver anniversary and the Golden Jubilee, their ages and addresses at the time. We need the names of the people who took part in scavenger hunts at each event. The items stolen. Also the ones returned or never recovered. Was there any property damage attributed to the pranks? I think that'll do for a start."

He sat forward. "But most important," he said, now very focused, "we need to detail the events surrounding the girl who disappeared from the fiftieth and drowned."

The banquet manager paled visibly, her hands trembling as she stood. "I think I saw one of our board members heading for the tennis courts a few minutes ago. Please wait here, Detective. Ms. Cutler."

Eighteen

Make tomorrow a new start: Take all the pains of the past
and all the disappointments—then pack them in a bag and
throw them in the river.   —AMERICAN PROVERB

"They'll soon learn," I whispered, "that you can't toss
somebody into the ocean and go about your business as if
nothing happened. Not forever, at least."

Werner raised a brow my way, but he said nothing.

Elation and energy zephyred through me. Lists, answers,
they were all forthcoming.

Or so I thought

Time grew long. Werner made a few notes. I got up to
pace and found myself near the open door of the room.

If said board member came to play tennis, he kept in his
locker a custom tailored little number in the most exquisite
of fabrics, straight from London's Savile Row. Had he
donned it now, just to intimidate the plebs?

I saw only his navy pinstripe back at first, as he and
the banquet manager conversed a distance away from the
open door in the hall. And I was duly intimidated, until he

glanced our way and back. He would never admit it, but he was Mr. Odd Duck, in the flesh, the man who stood on the sidewalk outside my shop Friday morning—which seemed like a lifetime ago. Why was he there? Did he know what might have been found?

"He's gonna be a big help," I whispered as Werner joined me and saw who I was looking at.

Werner coughed. "Not."

"Not," I echoed in a whisper. The closer he came, the stronger my sense that this was so not the man to ask about the girl who jumped in the ocean.

"Detective Werner," he said, "I'm the club's chairman of the board, Thatcher McDowell, CEO of East Connecticut Sailor's Bank. What can I do for you and your associate today?"

Zavier and Eric's father. I should have known.

He had to recognize me from yesterday. Unless he had lousy vision. Then again, maybe he did and that's why he didn't remember me speeding by him after I'd ransacked his carriage house. Bad eyes, that was it. I'd take what I could get.

Sleuthing-wise, however, I call this turn of events a brick wall. Get out of my way, power man in power suit running the show. Sure, his bank was started in East Connecticut for struggling sailors, a fact that their ads milked for emotion. But ECS banks could now be found all over the world, at the top of the food chain, as it were, eating little banks like M&M'S. And this big, powerful man, who had stood across from my shop looking as if he didn't want something to happen, presided over them all, including kazillions of dollars that billions of little people thought was actually theirs.

He controlled the Mystick by the Sea Country Club, too.

He stood about six and a half feet tall, so he towered over both of us. You'd think that his height and suit would make the detective look both dowdy and small. But at six feet, Detective Werner exuded the manly presence and self-confidence of his position.

As for that presence . . . on the day I came home from New York to open my vintage dress shop and Werner and I became reacquainted, he wore a discount rack suit. But now he dressed in classic styles of good fabric, because I helped him shop wisely.

I hated to admit that I'd been both a good and bad influence on the detective, which might serve him well in this case, as he and Mr. McDowell Sr. sized each other up.

As for me, I held my own in Dior's revolutionary New Look of 1947. My cinched-waist, soldier-blue wool coat matched my mini pleat dress. The paler pleats of the dress lined the standing shawl collar and peeked from the coat's waist. My outfit was worth at least three times as much as McDowell Sr.'s, and I think he knew it.

"If you don't mind having a seat, Mr. McDowell," Werner said, as if this were his turf—a bold, positive move. "I'll need you to answer a few questions."

The country club board rep folded his hand over a cane, and I noted the scar on one hand that continued down between thumb and index finger.

It made me wonder about those whose hands had bled for breaking window glass that fateful night.

"I understand your purpose, Detective," McDowell said. "And I speak for the entire board when I say that we're willing to cooperate with your investigation in every way. We will call for a closed-board meeting tomorrow night, with legal counsel present, and we invite you to attend and present your questions. Sadly, not you, Ms. Cutler."

"Sadly," I echoed. *Clearly he was saddened—not.* "But why do you need a lawyer if the crimes were committed *against* you, as representing the country club?" I asked, going for innocence and failing.

Ah, he allowed a bare flash of a pained expression. He'd had practice hiding his emotions, but he had not perfected his skill. Now I had my answer.

Did he know that I knew he'd been at my roof-raising, and that I'd caught his focused panic?

Thatcher McDowell schooled his features and smiled. "As vaguely as our banquet manager outlined your questions when she came for me a few minutes ago, I deem it prudent to make certain that in the ensuing investigation, the country club is not considered liable in any way. Especially given the death of that poor Robin O'Dowd."

"Outlined to you by the banquet manager that vaguely, was it?" I firmed my lips for a minute to let my words sink in. "Robin O'Dowd?" I added. "She must have been around the same age as your son Eric."

Some unseen force shoved a ramrod up McDowell's . . . spine . . . so he straightened and stared over the top of my head. "Detective," he said, addressing Werner behind me. "Membership to the country club is indeed the stuff of legend, passed most often from father to son, much like our legacy memberships are. This interview is at an end." He wrapped his big hand around the doorknob, an indication that we should precede him through the already-open door. "Until tomorrow night," he said. "Nine. Here at the club."

"Stop pouting, Mad," Werner said as we left the club, its bright green lawns a testament to its groundskeepers.

"I know, Werner, that this is a murder investigation. I know you figured it out, but you should know that I did, too. Two seconds, and he gives us the name and skinny on the dead girl?"

"I noticed that. Dead giveaway. Pardon the pun noir."

"More like a cover-up," I snipped.

"Sorry you can't be there. But really, Mad, you've become something of a squad mascot who gets the occasional great idea."

"Hah! I'm so proud, I'd stamp my foot if I could afford to break a Vivier heel."

He cupped the back of his neck with a hand. "You are pretty tricked out."

"I won't take 'tricked out' to mean 'in a clownish fashion.'"

He arched a brow. "I mean, why dress so fine to help solve a crime?"

I tilted my head. "Because if that man can dress in suits from London's Savile Row, his wife darned well can afford to shop at my shop."

"You little hustler." Pride belied his words.

"Scrap silk and little bone buttons! Businesswomen are not referred to as hustlers these days. I'm skillfully savvy and no slouch in the marketing department."

"You've got a heck of a Taser arm on you, too, not to mention your dexterity with indigo-blue pepper spray."

"How rude of you to mention my mistaken attacks on you."

The air between us became charged with sexual tension, because my Taser arm had led, circuitously, to our first thermonuclear kiss. No memory for me to haul out now, I told myself, as I checked the time on my vintage Lady Hamilton watch. "Well, that didn't take long. I guess I can go back and unveil the outfits Aunt Fiona sent to my shop this morning."

"What's the point?"

"I told you. I promised to judge them. The owners of the outfits I pick get to participate in the country club's *This Is Your Life* segment at the upcoming Very Vintage Valentine ball. You know, the winner gets his or her life read, and gets surprised with people from his or her past. Everybody wanted in. Dad and Aunt Fiona only have time for five, so they had to devise a fair way to eliminate people."

"Do you have an escort for the event?" Werner asked, opening my Element's door after I unlocked it with the remote.

"Of course I don't. My ex is in Europe." He waited until every bit of my vintage outfit was safe inside before he closed me in.

"I'll rent a tux. You can help me pick it out."

I rolled down my window. "Thank you, Detective. I'd love to go to the Very Vintage Valentine ball with you. We'll request a couple of rock and roll songs."

He tipped his hat and winked. "Good day, Ms. Cutler."

"You'll share your clues?" I called as he turned away.

He stopped and nodded, barely turning his head. "Perhaps, since you expressed it as a request and not an order."

"I did tell you that the outfits I'm going back to the shop to judge were all worn to the fiftieth jubilee?"

He turned back to me. "Not today you didn't. You might have yesterday, but it didn't resonate then." He furrowed his brow. "Because we covered several other, more important subjects then. And yet I find that anything to do with the Golden Jubilee interests me a great deal at this point. Scene of the crime and all that."

"Care to join us at the shop?"

"Exactly who is 'us'?"

"I'm calling Aunt Fee and Eve to help me. Mrs. Meyers will leave when I get back, but I'm not sure about Dolly and Ethel."

He chuckled. "I've noticed that they act as if Vintage Magic is their own private country club."

"If I'd had to pay full price . . . I shudder to think. Dolly practically handed it to me on a silver platter. You know that, right?"

"I get your drift. It's her country club if she wants it to be."

"So, wanna come see some outfits worn that night? I hear that as many men entered the competition as women."

"You've reeled me in."

We both winked, and as he got in his car, I realized I was smiling. A smile that remained as I called Eve. Fiona was on her way to meet me, Eve said, and she made me promise not to start without her. She'd come right after class.

Werner pulled his car alongside mine, driver's window to driver's window. "If you're ordering takeout, I'll have Chinese."

"Okay. We can eat before we open the garment bags. Wanna pick up the food? You get to pick what we eat." I rifled through my purse and hung a fifty dollar bill out the window.

He took it, focused on it, growled, and dropped it back inside my window.

"Great, now I'm gonna have to crawl around on the floor to find it."

Werner's grin grew. "That I'd like to see. Lunch is on me. I could hear your stomach growling in the country club. First, though, I need to stop at the courthouse to pick up some paperwork. Please wait to go fishing for that bill until I get back."

"Lunch for at least four, maybe five. And, Lytton?"

"Yes, Madeira?"

"Why do you think McDowell wanted a lawyer?" I hesitated about giving away my thoughts, but only for a minute. "His kids would have been the right age to participate in that scavenger hunt."

"I've noticed that men in expensive suits like his have a special way of squirming," Werner said. "I caught the tick in his cheek. If I hadn't thought there was a crime before speaking to him, I would think so now. And you're right. It's worse than we thought. Robin O'Dowd was a murder victim whose death was pronounced accidental. Her case needs reopening, and about time."

Satisfaction rushed through my veins, and my eyes widened involuntarily.

"We hit pay dirt, Mad. Now all we have to do is be careful not to damage the landscape or alert the natives while we dig."

Nineteen

Eve, Dolly, and Ethel were waiting for me when I got back to the shop. Fee had left to bring Mrs. Meyers home.

My three friends looked pretty guilty.

"What did you do? Did you open the garment bags?"

"Of course not," Eve said. "You said not to."

"Then what are you all hiding?"

"It's about a blog," Eve said.

"A blog?" That was the last thing I'd expected to hear. "Who cares about a silly blog?"

"This one's not silly," Dolly said. "I've been reading it the past few days. It's called Vintage Dirt by someone who calls himself the Mystick Falls Masque. Seems to be a rabble rouser who outs local secrets. I believe it's relatively new. I can't identify the two people with their heads together in that grainy picture at the top, but I once wore clothes like theirs."

"Dolly, will you print out the page with the grainy picture for me?" I asked.

"Oh, I did, dear." She fished it out of her bright orange Jaclyn-ette purse—square, stand-up, very seventies—and handed it to me.

"Yep, grainy." Without one identifiable face, so I'd have to study it for clues. I slipped it into my pocket. "Thanks."

"I'm lucky the Internet wasn't around when I had my fiery fling with Dante," Dolly proclaimed or bragged.

And somewhere nearby, I heard him chuckle.

"Mama!" Ethel snapped, foolishly shocked. "You didn't *really* do all that?"

"I did everything everybody ever said and more." Dolly's pride was as genuine as the rose in her cheeks and the gleam in her eyes.

"Let's get back to this blog, shall we?" I asked. "Eve? I assume you're the one who found it."

"No, dear," Dolly said. "It was an anonymous tip we got on your shop phone about fifteen minutes ago. Someone told me to 'write this down,' so I did."

"A web address?" I asked, and gave it to Eve. She looked it up on my computer.

"Was the anonymous caller a man or a woman?" I asked Dolly.

"Yes. Well, I couldn't tell, not at all. It sounded more like a robot."

"Gotta love the technological age," I said.

Eve turned the monitor to face us, so we could read it. "The headline is 'Just Dug Up.'"

"That sounds grisly." I read it to myself, and then I read

it out loud. " 'Just between us and the roof rafters,' " it says, " 'the long-lost cash box belonging to a certain country club known for keeping its members squeaky clean—even if they reek—turned up again like a bad penny. Like nine hundred thousand bad pennies come back to bite the greedy, soulless rich brats who done a whole lot of some-bodies wrong.' "

I shook my head. "It's both cryptic and damn near incriminating."

"Makes no sense to me," Ethel said.

"It sort of does to me," I admitted, and continued. " 'In this phantom reporter's opinion, somebody should fry.' "

Dolly *tsk*ed. "That's harsh."

But I thought that whoever had written this knew the whole story, including Robin O'Dowd and why she ended in the ocean in a storm. "Okay," I said. "Here's more of the blog: 'This rover is here to reveal what will soon come out anyway. Said country club confidentially reported to their insurance company that the amount they lost in the rob-bery was precisely double the actual loss.' "

I whooped. "A good case of insurance fraud will make the country club, aka Mr. Holier Than Thou McDowell Sr., accountable," I said. "That's my opinion, not the blog's." I paused, then continued reading. " 'But don't focus on the lar-ceny, find Robin's O'Dowd's murderer.' " Now if, as a result of dredging all this up, we *could* find Robin's murderer, or murderers, and make them pay . . . Not that we knew for sure that it was murder. Except that the Masque said so.

Dolly elbowed me. "Keep reading."

"Oh. Sorry. 'Said high-and-mighty club also reported

confidentially to the charity due to get the proceeds of the event that the amount stolen was precisely half the actual loss, and they gave the charity half of that, after deducting expenses . . . of course.' "

Fiona whistled, surprising me with her presence. "Sounds like trouble," she said.

"It is. . . for the country club. You can read the whole blog after I finish."

Dolly hooted. "I like a good scandal to keep the juices flowing. Read, Mad, read."

"'Kay. 'Who took possession of the money the insurance company paid out? This roving reporter would like to know. Because it is not accounted for on a certain country club's books. Detective Werner and Ms. Cutler' "—that took my breath away—" 'you were in the right place today. Keep digging. Why not start in the basement?' "

I rubbed my arms against the goose pimples and shivers the last sentence brought.

"Mad, they named you," Ethel said, excited for me.

I felt nauseous. "I don't like that 'this roving reporter' knows what I'm doing."

Dolly wagged her finger at me. "Take it from somebody with experience. Don't do anything you don't want talked about. See, I mostly worked at making the gossips happy," Dolly bragged. "And if you don't want that, then sneak around real good. Want some tips?"

"Not right now, Dolly," Fiona said. "Mad has to finish reading that blog."

"Oh, right." I touched my brow. "I think I was blocking it. Brace yourself. Here goes. It says, 'Detective, lining the pockets of the rich with hundred dollar bills has always been big in some circles. Ask whoever's in charge you-know-where. Maybe you'll get answers, but don't count on the truth. Tell us this: Who takes part in these scavenger hunts, and who dies? This is Mystick Falls' phantom blogger, signing off.'"

"Whoa!" I said, sitting down hard in front of the computer. "This is big. Who would know that Werner and I went to the country club this morning? Or even that Isaac found a cash box in my rafters two days ago? I just turned it in to the police yesterday." Or that someone, namely Robin, had died.

"Everybody in town saw Isaac find the box," Aunt Fee said.

"That's a grudge blog," Dolly added.

Ethel harrumphed. "Like you know what a blog is."

"Unlike you, who lives in the dark ages, I turn on the computer every morning and surf the net. You may not move with the times, but I do. I follow several interesting blogs. I even have friends on the social sites."

Ethel raised her nose in the air and went for her coat and purse.

I sighed. "Okay, I have to think."

I paced while Eve scanned the blog. "Looks like we have some sleuthing to do," she said. "Seems more fun now that there's a phantom blogger roving around watching you."

I elbowed her and glanced back at the Sweets, who were both packing up.

Fiona held her car keys, ready to take them home. "There are a few more garment bags than we expected," Fee said. "Your father helped bring them earlier, and he said to remind you that this wasn't his idea." She opened the door for the Sweets. "Be back in a jiff. Anything you want?"

"Lunch?" Eve asked.

"Never mind, Werner's bringing Chinese food." I primped the holly, ivy, and white mums set in a sculptured red Lucite box bag with a cracked top. Since I couldn't bring myself to throw away damaged purses, I used them to hold flower arrangements.

In this case, I truly mourned the bag. According to Judith Miller's book *Handbags*, this particular bag would be worth a grand in perfect condition. I kept hoping I'd find one with a cracked body and could operate to turn the two good halves into one awesome purse.

I checked my messages, made a couple of notes to call people back, then continued around the counter, which was backed by the wall that separated my shopping area to the right of the front door from the lounge area and dressing room to the left.

The garment bags were behind the wall, in an open space between the beverage cart and the art deco sitting area, through which my customers passed to get to the fitting room. It's so wide open, I had once roller-skated around back there with my fashion intern, but that's a story for another day.

I stopped dead at the sight. "How many racks of garment bags is that?"

"Eleven racks," Eve said. "Fiona was nervous that there were so many, so I'm glad she wasn't here to see your reaction."

"Are you kidding me?"

"No, she's really upset about the sheer volume."

Fiona cleared her throat behind us.

One look at her and I knew I couldn't change my mind, so I had to find a way to make it easier on myself. I reached over and squeezed her hand. "It'll be okay. I'll figure it out."

I tapped my lips with a finger. "First step, remove the garment bags and drop them in that corner across from the stairs for now."

Vainglory's gown was in about the fifth bag to get unzipped and removed.

"Hey," Eve said in surprise. "That backasswards-type apron thingy looks like it might match the design on the fabric wrapped around the—*pfft!*" She lost her breath, with my help.

I'd shoved an armful of garment bags in Eve's face to shut her up. I didn't want anyone else to connect the cash box wrapping to the dress I planned to pick in my official capacity as judge, for my own personal sleuthing reasons. Though I fervently hoped that justice would be served by the choice. "Eve, help me bring these into the dressing rooms, will you?"

Twenty

A sea of funereal black dresses saddens the paparazzi to no end. Explore gowns in jewel tones or pastel hues if you're usually more inclined to darker shades.

—JANIE BRYANT, *THE FASHION FILE*

Eve was still miffed when we got to the dressing rooms, the horse stalls in Dante's day.

"I know it matches," I told Eve. "I saw in my vision that it matched. Why do you think I agreed to judge this foolish contest in the first place?"

"Oh. Oh no! These clothes are going to give you visions, aren't they? Tons of them. Hey, did you and Werner open that box? What was in it?"

"You wouldn't believe me if I told you."

"Try me."

I gave her the abbreviated version.

"I don't believe you."

"There you go."

"So it was like . . . a robbery?"

"A scavenger hunt, where the scavengers *intended* to

return the goods, but did I forget to tell you about the girl who drowned?"

"Scrap, not a ghost. Please tell me that you haven't taken to speaking to ghosts."

"Not on a subject I'd choose," I said for Dante's sake, feeling a whisper of a touch on my cheek. Holy eyelet, he was toying with me.

When I stepped into my bathroom, I knew it. Two names were written, presumably by Dante, on the glass in my best and most expensive lipstick. I cleaned it off and didn't know whether to be grateful for the names, though I couldn't be sure they fit the picture, or furious because he'd just cost me a fortune in lipstick.

I left the bathroom with Eve behind me demanding ghostly details. I stopped so the others couldn't hear us. "You're coming sleuthing with me. I'll have a chance to tell you everything then."

"Are we gonna live dangerously?"

"I hope not."

"Mad, you take all the fun out of sleuthing. Where are we going?"

"An abandoned mill near the ocean and railroad tracks, which gives me an idea of its location."

"Great. When?"

"Once I figure out where, Noodle. Time, the middle of the night. Now shh."

We got in our best trouble in the middle of the night, Eve and I.

Eve slapped my arm with a chuckle. "Noodle. I like it."

"You two keep peeling off the garment bags," I told Eve

and Fee. "Sorting will be easier without the bags. Put menswear on a separate rack. I'm guessing five to one, gowns to tuxes. I doubt I'll choose any black gowns, but if one stands out, I'll need to see them. Rack them by colors as best you can. Keep outfits with labels separated from outfits without. Got it?"

Fiona saluted, military style.

Eve chose an alternate salute. "What are you going to do?" she asked.

"I need to go make notes on how to approach the situation."

"Madeira Cutler," Fiona said. "Are you sleuthing again?"

"Fee, you're one with my dad now, and frankly, I'd rather you didn't know the answer to that. Better you shouldn't keep anything from him, right?"

A lovely soft smile transformed her expression.

"Of course, right," I said, since she'd lost track of my question.

I left them to do their thing while I made a "to sleuth" list.

Since the case of Robin O'Dowd, the drowned swimmer, sat heavily on my mind, I noted whom I hoped Werner and I could investigate together and what Eve and I had to handle in a more clandestine manner. For Eve and me: Find more pieces of the petticoat.

First we'd need that list of people who'd attended both jubilees, twenty-fifth and fiftieth, which Werner had already asked for. But—I picked up the phone and speed-dialed him.

"Parking at Chinese takeout right now," he said as he picked up.

"You need to send a crime-scene contingent to investigate the basement of the country club," I said.

"I saw the blog," he said. "A blog is not strong enough motivation for a search warrant."

"Cold grommets and toothy metal zippers, why not?"

"Sorry, Mad."

I huffed, thinking about how Eve and I might do some sleuthing down in that particular basement, and I shivered, which probably meant we shouldn't. "Stud, you need to call the country club back. We forgot to ask for group pictures from the events, though individual pics would be better. They always have professional photographers for that purpose, and I'd bet the country club keeps a set from every event."

"Stud?"

"You rather be a wiener?"

"Stud it is. I can ask the country club board tomorrow night when I meet with them and their lawyers for all the lists and pictures you want."

"No, ask them right now, so they have them ready for you tomorrow night."

"When did you become my boss?"

"You heard Mr. Moneybags, aka Thatcher McDowell Sr. I'm your associate. Just a little more efficient and faster-acting than you, that's all. You're the brains, I'll give you that."

Werner harrumphed. "I know a snow job when I hear one, but you're good at it, I'll give you that."

"Oh, and make it clear that the rosters should include maiden names, former addresses, and current addresses, so we can further investigate. You might need a subpoena or search warrant-whatchamajiggie."

"Bye, Mad."

Hmm, I thought, looking at my dead cell phone. I'd have to be cleverer when I needed something from now on. Straightforward made me sound bossy. Clever was the route I needed to adopt, and maybe a little bit flirty, though not too flirty—a fine line for me, especially with Werner. And I would have to be careful not to cross it.

Eve and Fiona were making too much noise and having too much fun without me. So I put everything about the case in its own folder, tucked it into a file drawer, and joined them.

"Oh, this is a vintage-dress lover's dream," I said. "Even the black gowns have their fair share of prizes."

I went right to the men's formals. "Only one uniform entered?" I asked.

"Only one."

"Put an empty rack on that side of the room for the six we choose, and hang the uniform there. It's number one. Aunt Fee, my appointment book is on the counter. Can you schedule him for a fitting now? I don't want to have them all at once.

"And, Fiona, we'll have to set up a display of evening bags. I've got a store of beaded clutches from the forties and fifties upstairs. Make sure you bring down certain brands: Corde Bead, Magid, Grandee Bead, Rochette, Whiting & Davis, and that beautiful little shell of a Valerie Stevens. People who are attending have bought out the old display."

"Will do. So glad to help. Your father and I would feel better if you didn't end up stressed over this."

"Now, Eve." I lifted Chakra into my arms; she'd been leaping around the room, swiping at tulle skirts and rolling beneath them, as if she were chasing butterflies through a meadow. "Let's choose five more outstanding formals."

Twenty-one

I see myself as a true modernist. Even when I do a traditional gown, I give it a modern twist. I go to the past for
research. I need to know what came before so I can break
the rules.   —VERA WANG

Excitement rushed through me just looking at the vintage
formals I found myself privileged to be able to handle. I
was a sucker for antique clothing, and here were samples of
the world's greatest waiting for me to decide the fates of
their owners.

"Aunt Fee, please tell the five people whose outfits we
choose to bring me, or give you, pictures of their outfit
being worn at the Golden Jubilee. Some people may have
already given you photos. I know you showed me pics
when you asked me to judge the contest. Just to prove
someone wore it that night and nobody's trying to slip in a
ringer. To be fair to everyone who entered."

"That's easy," Aunt Fee said. "Everyone posed for a professional photographer beside a sign marking the event."

"I thought so. But just in case, let's choose a few
alternates."

Eve huffed to get my attention, and she crossed her arms over her stomach like she might be sick. To be fair, she did look a bit green around the gills. "Mad," she begged, "don't touch any of these outfits, please? For me?"

"Sweetie, are you sick?" I asked.

"No, just scared."

"Geez, so you scare me back? Begging is not your style, but you're good at it! I know better than to touch the clothes; don't worry. It'll be bad enough when and if I have to fit or alter any of the outfits." Of course, I wanted to read the embroidered peach crepe silk, Vainglory's gown, again. I couldn't wait to check out Deborah VanCortland's past.

Eve stopped unzipping a garment bag and turned on a boot heel. "You mean the owners, right? Fit them to the owners?"

"No," I said, "the requirement is an outfit worn at the Golden Jubilee. This year's wearer won't necessarily be that year's owner."

Eve bit her lip. "It's true. Prime vintage does change hands. I guess that makes sense."

"What's up, Fiona?" I asked. "Eve looks sick, you look worried."

"I am, or was, about you reading these things, but you seem to have made peace with the possibility."

"Let's just say that I have an ulterior motive for taking the chance, and leave it at that."

Fiona raised a stop-right-there hand. "I know nothing."

"I'm glad we understand each other. Please remind non–*This Is Your Life*rs, when you return their entries, that they should wear these to the ball to qualify for a prize. I can tell with one look, though I haven't seen labels, that we're surrounded with prize-winning pieces."

Fiona scanned the room. "It's true, and I'm so glad you reminded me. I'm feeling positively fa-la-la giddy, I'm so excited about our part in the Valentine's ball."

"Chinese food's here," Werner announced.

"Smells delicious," I said. "Be with you in a minute. I'm more than pleased with the uniform. One down, five to go."

"Sounds easy," Eve said, opening the stapled bags of food while Fiona took out plastic plates and utensils.

Werner sort of growled, caught my right hand in his, and dragged me away from my checkout/lunch counter and into the dressing rooms, where he backed me into a stall.

His hands on the wall beside my head, he stood up close and personal. "It's time to leave high school behind."

"I've been thinking the same thing."

My phone buzzed in a text.

I read a message from Nick that needed no reply, and gave it to Werner to read. "'Cupcake,'" he read aloud. "'Put on your designer panties, the red lace ones, and be yourself. Have fun. Rock 'n' Roll to your heart's content.'"

"Permission?"

"Guilt?"

Werner raised a brow as his frown turned to a grin. "Red lace?"

"Uh-hmm."

"I prefer an electric blue, myself."

"I'll replace them."

He growled low in his throat, brought his lips to mine, hungry, almost as hungry as me, and we made an unbounded thermonuclear meal of each other.

"Mad," Eve called. "You're being conspicuous by your absence, both of you."

"We need to talk," Werner said.

"Or kiss some more?" I asked.

"Oh, that, too." And he complied.

"Everybody will wonder what we're doing in here."

"We know what you're doing in there," Aunt Fiona called loudly. "You're talking, like your father and I do."

My laughter ended the kiss.

Werner pulled a bit away, but not much. "I'm calling for a replay. Later. My house." His lips tickled mine as he spoke.

"You're on," I said. "We have to go back to the lunch crowd." So we did, arm in arm.

"Nick's text was almost psychic," Werner said.

"He's seen us together." I stopped walking. "You believe in psychics?"

"Sure."

Wow, did I have a story for him . . . someday.

Werner raised our clasped hands, kissed my knuckles, and eyed me like a prime rib. I had a whole-body reaction.

"For the record," I said, my stomach growling, "I sensed that Nick and Paisley needed to give the kind of blessing they'd like to receive, and I intend to give it to them."

"You sensed it, did you? That doesn't surprise me."

Fiona and Eve hooted as we rounded the wall behind the counter where they waited impatiently. "Good veggie pot stickers," Eve said, pointing to her chipmunk cheeks.

"Glad to be of assistance, Ms. Cutler," Werner said to me with a grin. "Anytime." He winked at me. "Anytime." And he tipped back a Dos Equis, while I watched, sort of mesmerized. This having permission to watch and everything, was heady stuff. It allowed for all kinds of acceptance and hope. Until this second, I hadn't realized I'd been holding back. "Wait, did you buy dessert, Lytton? 'Cause I smell chocolate."

"Nope."

Mom, then. Telling me I'd finally hit my mark. Werner.

"I need to go underwear shopping," I said to no one in particular, though Werner stopped drinking to eye me, and Fiona and Eve giggled and elbowed each other.

I guessed I'd been sort of down since Nick's disappearance into the worldly jaws of the FBI. They were glad to see me come out of it.

The bell above the door tinkled, and a woman with a garment bag came in. "They said at the country club that it wasn't too late to get this outfit to you because the entries just got here today?" She'd phrased it in the form of a question, behind which I heard an unspoken, *Did I make it, did I, did I, huh? Huh?*"

"Bambi-Jo," I said, recognizing her voice immediately.

I got double takes all around, and wished shrinking to invisibility was an option.

"Do I know you?" a stumped Bambi-Jo asked.

Stupid, stupid, stupid. "Ah, somehow, at some point, I got a visual of the fiftieth. Pictures, I suppose. Guess I remembered because your name's so unique. You don't seem to have changed at all." *Of course, I couldn't really see you. I just huddled there inside you.* They would put me in a padded cell for that admission.

Bambi barked a laugh. "I've changed forty years' worth, but thanks."

And she'd found her strong voice, though I'd had a peek of the meek girl when she asked about her entry.

I'd thought she and I were kindred spirits and could be friends . . . back when she had been my age. Now she was old enough to be my mother. I introduced her all around and accepted the garment bag, which I handed to Eve, her eyes round, pupils dilated; she so knew I'd goofed because I saw this woman in a vision.

Fiona's head tilt said she suspected as well.

Werner looked confused, and before we stepped beyond underwear-shopping, he needed to know everything, and I mean everything, about the psychic, daughter-of-a-witch me.

That's how I'd gotten Nick and Werner mixed up. Nick knew and accepted facts. Just the facts, ma'am—a regular Joe Friday, letter-of-the-law kind of guy. The high school jock who liked the rush of crowds cheering; a great catch for a Cutler girl. Now outgrown by a Cutler woman. Paisley, or someone like her, if Nick ever stopped to choose a mate, would heap praise on him and polish his medals. She'd travel the world with him, as hungry for adventure as he. Whoever Nick Jaconetti chose would live *his* life.

I had to live my own.

I'd gone to grammar school with my choice; he'd baited me, and I'd called him Wiener.

He knew and embraced the essence of Madeira Cutler, even the brat, and he wanted the real me beside him, here in Mystic and as far away as Mystick Falls. I knew that deep in my soul.

Bambi-Jo cleared her throat. I turned back to her. "It's a wide-skirted gown, right?" I said. "Did you bring the crinoline?"

"Ah, no," Bambi-Jo said. "I thought if my gown was chosen, I'd bring the crinoline for the fitting."

Aunt Fiona cleared her throat. "I'm sorry, Bambi-Jo, but you're disqualified. Madeira, here, is our judge, and she's not supposed to know who the formals belong to."

I turned to Fee. "I only remember the Southern belle–type hoopskirt, nothing more, and we have a lot of those back there. I have no recollection of even the color. Just take it out while I'm not looking, hide it among the stock we haven't perused, and I won't know the difference."

Bambi-Jo hugged me. "That's so sweet of you. Thanks."

Werner became the detective again. "Excuse me, Miss—?"

"My last name is Zeller," she supplied. "You can call me Miss Zeller."

"Miss Zeller," he repeated. "I'd like to ask you a few questions, but since I'm speaking for the law, you have a right to an attorney. Just say so and we'll put off the questioning until you can have an attorney present."

"No, that's . . ." She sighed. "I don't need an attorney. Ask away."

"Did you by any chance take part in the widely publicized scavenger hunt at the Mystick by the Sea's fiftieth jubilee?"

Bambi-Jo paled to the color of wallpaper paste. Her shoulders sagged for a minute, but her chin came up. "Yes, I took part." She held out her wrists. "Forty years is too long to keep a secret. Just arrest me and get it over with."

"That won't be necessary," Werner said after a good eye-to-eye with the woman, "but I retain the right to question you, and you retain the right to a lawyer. Fiona, do you have her name and address, since Mad says this event is yours?"

"Yes, Detective, I have it. Sorry, Miss Zeller. But it wouldn't be a conflict of interest if you retained me as your lawyer. I became a judge and retired, but I can still represent you."

Bambi-Jo gave Fiona a grateful nod. "For everyone's information, I discreetly returned what I scavenged years ago, Detective. My conscience is clear, if not my memories."

Werner gave a noncommittal nod. "You're not under suspicion. Yet."

So, she had done the right thing, so . . . one less piece of the petticoat puzzle to solve. "If your gown doesn't get chosen for *This Is Your Life*, don't forget that you can still wear it to the ball, and that I do alterations. I think you're a bit thinner than I remember in the picture."

Bambi raised a brow. "I think you need glasses."

"Miss Zeller, you'll call me at the Mystick Falls police station within the next forty-eight hours to make an appointment, and bring Fee, I mean Ms. Sullivan, with you as legal counsel. If you don't, you'll find a couple of black-and-whites at your door. Not that I'm accusing you of anything. But we need to talk. Do we understand each other?"

Bambi blew out a long, slow breath. "I didn't do anything wrong except run with the wrong crowd."

Werner raised a brow. "Which doesn't mean that you don't know anything."

Bambi gave a sick squeak. "Strictly speaking, I don't know what happened that night, nothing dire, anyway. But you may understand something that I didn't. Wind me up and I never shut up, that's the only warning I'll give you."

She closed her hand around the doorknob. "I wanted to hang with the rich, popular clique forty years ago. Stupid pride. Today, I should have accepted that I missed the deadline. Still with the pride, don'tcha know?" She turned to me. "You'd think I would have learned."

"The detective would have found you within the week," I said. "He's reopened the Robin O'Dowd case."

"It's a case?"

"A murder investigation," Werner said.

Bambi's eyes filled. "I never wanted to hear those words. I was so afraid."

"Why didn't you come forward then?"

"I was a nobody. Me? Against all that money power? No way. Not unless I wanted to get run out of town. Or worse." She eyed Werner. "I look forward to talking to you. I think." She nodded and left.

The minute the door clicked shut behind her, Werner looked at me with narrowed eyes—like, if he were wearing glasses, he would be looking at me over them—mouth firm. "And you, Madeira? You just happened to know her name?"

"Remember that I said we have to talk? Well, I don't need legal counsel, but maybe we should get a couple six-packs of Dos Equis before we do."

"Underwear shopping first, then we talk," he said. "There's nothing you can say to scare me away."

"That's what you think," Eve said.

Fiona silently seemed to agree, though her eyes weren't half as wide as Eve's.

I could tell from Werner's expression that he'd guessed, from our earlier conversation in the dressing room, that I might have some kind of psychic ability. But he sure hadn't guessed the witch part.

And I'd thought that choosing the formals was going to be the hard part of this assignment.

Twenty-two

"Okay, lunch, everyone," I said in all innocence. "Lytton, you want to get two extra barstools from the closet beneath the stairs?"

Fee and Eve had thrown a plastic tablecloth over my countertop and set out everything. "Nobody goes anywhere near the costumes in the back from this moment on," I declared. "We'll eat right here, then everybody helps disinfect and clean the counter, then we all take a shower before we touch the formals again."

"Together?" Werner and Eve asked.

"Go ahead," I said, "if the two of you so desire."

Eve made a strangled sound and Werner paled.

Fiona patted his cheek. "Silly boy," she said. "Hunky, but silly."

"Do I smell lemon chicken?" I checked the containers.

156

"Oh, and pad thai noodles. They are so much better than lo mein. You know what I like, Detective."

"Not everything, but I'm an eager pupil and a quick study."

"Please," Eve said, "you're testing my gag reflexes."

"It's the peanut sauce," Aunt Fee said, pretending innocence as she took some for herself.

We settled at the counter, quiet at first, savoring the range of tastes: lemon, ginger, peanut sauce. "Lytton?" I asked. "What did you have to pick up at the courthouse? Is it for the country club case?"

"As a matter of fact, yes. I collected copies of the paperwork declaring Robin O'Dowd dead. It's a matter of public record, so I can repeat it, but I wouldn't want it to become fodder for a blog, say. Especially not now."

If only Werner knew what Eve and Fiona had kept to themselves since my psychometry had come into play, and I started zoning at the touch of vintage clothes and investigating misdeeds on my own, with or without police approval. "I promise you, they can be trusted."

Werner nodded, seemingly satisfied that they understood. "It seems that Robin O'Dowd's brother, Wayne, and his wife, Wynona, had Robin declared legally dead seven years to the day after she was reported washed into the ocean by a rogue wave."

So Robin's brother had married Wynona, aka Lady Backroom? "Robin drowned on the night of the country club's Golden Jubilee, right?" I confirmed, refilling my plate.

Werner did the same. "Actually, the time her friends reported the wave taking her was after midnight, so her date of death is listed as the day after the fiftieth."

"That almost complicates the issue, doesn't it? I mean, the country club can wash their hands of it, can't they? Unless it was on their land."

Werner gave a half nod. "It was on their land."

I snapped my head up on that. "Now, see. I find that hard to believe."

"Why?" Werner asked. "Because Thatcher McDowell told us it wasn't on their land?"

"Their members were scavenger hunting, destroying property, even people, hiding objects"—I caught the questioning looks—"one imagines," I added, "when things have been scavenged. But that's not the point. Why go strolling along the shore at the very location you're desecrating?"

"I'd like to hear more about your imaginary scavenger hunt," Werner said, as he checked his watch and stood to leave. "Well," he said, cupping my neck and bringing my brow to his, "back to work." His fingers sifting down through the hair at my nape as he let me go made me shiver.

"I'll be here when you get back."

"Fee, Eve," he said. "Don't let her come to harm."

"We haven't yet," Fiona said.

"They know what you're gonna tell me, right?" he asked.

I nodded. "One or both of them always has my back."

He turned to them. "Thank you. You don't know how much I appreciate knowing that," he said. "You know how she is. She gets on a case and forgets she's not Wonder Woman."

That cut a bit close to the bone. "Gee," I said, tilting my head and furrowing my brows, "you mean I'm not?"

My protectors had the good grace to open ranks and let me in. They literally all turned toward me and invited me to join the conversation again.

I nodded my appreciation. "Lytton, does Robin's brother have motive?"

Werner shifted gears in a blink, and if he felt any discomfort at the affection for me that he'd revealed, I saw no sign of it. He jumped right back on the case, firmed his lips, and nodded. "About two years after Robin was declared dead, Wayne, his paternal grandparents' sole heir, inherited the family fortune. He got the docks, slips, warehouses, and more property than any one man could ever need. Since then, he's turned a lot of it into condos and made millions more doing it."

"Which is why double the inheritance worked so much better than half the inheritance," I snipped. "Sounds like motive to me," I continued, so glad he'd reopened the case. I didn't know why I felt this gut-deep imperative to find justice for Robin, but her case had gotten to me like no other. Maybe it was because she hadn't had closure, and neither had her family. Presumed dead. No body. No headstone to sit beside, no name carved in granite to trace and remember.

On the other hand, maybe the depth of my empathy is the precise reason her case became my universal mandate. Mine specifically.

I wasn't really throwing Robin's brother, or his wife, Wynona, to the wolves. Werner could easily disprove either of them as suspects, with my help, of course. What mattered was him looking for the reason she'd gone in the water that night. I wanted us to find the person, or persons, responsible. If in fact she hadn't gone in on her own.

"I guess we need to investigate Robin herself," I said. "I mean, suppose her life was unbearable and she jumped willingly into a storm-tossed sea?"

Truth was, I didn't think Wayne had been among the people at the warehouse that night, though Wynona had. Unless Wayne turned out to be Snake, the slimy one, or even Tuxman, the one who'd hid his loot in the pipes of a ramshackle mill.

On the other hand, Wayne's family had owned property on the docks, and we'd been in a dark seaside warehouse. Granted, the building had seemed empty and abandoned, but it wasn't, because there'd been no mistaking the fish smell. Could Wayne or his wife have been the brains behind his sister's drowning?

Well, not his wife. Wynona wasn't married to him back then, but maybe she wanted to be and Robin disapproved, or she wanted Robin's half of the money for herself as Wayne's wife.

I mean, how could you make someone dive into the ocean in a storm?

But no one had used the word "dive" in the belly of the whale that night, had they?

One could force someone into the water. Or push them in. Most easily done if the victim is unconscious. Or dead.

"Since I reopened this case because of the box your building crew found, I wish I could invite you to question Mr. and Mrs. O'Dowd with me," Werner said, "but I want them to know we mean business. So, I need to bring a couple of black-and-whites."

I swiveled on my stool, away from and then back toward

Werner. "You will tell me about questioning the O'Dowds later? I can keep my mouth shut."

"It's true, she can," Eve said. "Even when being tickled to within an inch of her life."

Werner chuckled. "I'll have to remember that. We have a lot to talk about tonight, Mad. Maybe it'd better be a sleepover."

Eve perked up. "Like last—"

"Not you, Eve. Just Mad. Me and Mad."

Butterflies took over my insides. This had started in third grade when he'd called me Glamazon and I'd called him Little Wiener. I wonder if we were attracted then. Yes, I'd maligned his manhood before I knew what manhood was. I was sorry for that, especially since the man's kisses now made my toes curl. It might be difficult to keep a straight face tonight, under the circumstances, but I was gonna give it my Wonder Woman best.

"I'd stay and babysit the shop if you needed her, Lytton," Eve said. "But, Mad, you shouldn't be surprised if, while you were gone, I tried on a few of those gowns in the back."

"If you tried them on and so much as popped a button," I told my BFF, "I would do worse than tickle you. I'd double dare you to wear red to the Valentine's ball."

Eve gave me a snobby chin up, but she spoiled it with an eye twinkle.

I hooked my arm through Werner's. "I'll walk you to the car, Detective. So we can go over your interview strategy."

Oh, I liked to bring out that grin of his.

One last thermonuclear kiss coming up.

Twenty-three

Fashion adjusts to the speed of the traffic, holds its own in
the adaptation to the rapid, fleeting appearance that alone
promises the attention, and the gaze, of those passing in
continual motion.   —SABINE FABO, 1998

I let myself into Werner's house through the kitchen door—
to the tantalizing aroma of a homemade Italian dinner—
and a hunk who made me drool more than the food did.

I'd carefully chosen a strapless electric-blue Versace
gown with a left-leg split, trimmed in black leather, like my
fashion-forward Ferragamo booties.

"My God, you're dazzling," he said, shirtsleeves rolled
up, dish towel over a shoulder, a stirring spoon in each
hand.

"Nothing retro for tonight," I said. "I'm making a fashion statement that I hope will take us from the present into
the future. Screw the past."

He dropped his spoons.

"Don't! No kissing until after dinner, and after I've
bared my soul."

"Sounds ominous. Will we ever get to the kissing part?"

"That'll be up to you."

"Glad I'll have a say in it. Can we talk while we eat—multitask, so to speak—get it all out there as soon as possible, let the kissing and disrobing begin?"

I laughed. How could such a hunk, such a strong-willed and, when necessary, hard-hearted detective also look like my own personal teddy bear? It would be difficult to keep my own ground rules.

We sat at the perfectly set round oak dining room table with Werner holding a meatball at the end of his fork while staring straight at my cleavage.

I took a deep breath, widening his eyes. "My mother was a witch," I said.

He twitched, trying not to react. The meatball fell off his fork, bounced, and landed in his lap.

I bit my lip on a giggle as he retrieved it. "She was Wiccan, but she was also a natural. I've inherited several of her gifts. I haven't embraced the Wiccan faith, but spells come to me in my sleep though I haven't cast any. I participated in a ritual at my dearest friend's funeral in New York and told myself I stood in my mother's place. Aunt Fiona and I, we cleansed the shop, once a morgue, of negativity, Wiccan style, before I moved in."

"Now can I touch you?"

"No. How do you feel about my paranormal ability? About me?"

"Horny. Wrong answer? I always knew you were special?"

I chuckled. "I'm psychic. Psychometric, actually."

"You read objects?"

His knowledge surprised me. "In my case, it's vintage

clothes. What I learn helps me sleuth. For some universal reason, my visions are always connected to, or they're the origination of, my sleuthing. Like the wrapping around the box. It's a petticoat piece that took me to the night the box was stolen."

Werner threw down his napkin. "Damn it, Madeira, I knew you had an edge. You always know so much about the cases we're working on."

"Are you mad?"

"Exonerated. I feel exonerated. I'm not a second-rate detective. You're a first-rate sleuth."

I started to reach for his hand but then pulled back. "You don't hate that I'm a natural witch, and psychic to boot?"

"I hate that we're on different sides of the table," he said.

"Aunt Fiona calls my readings universal mandates, like I'm supposed to help solve the mystery they bring me to, past or present."

"Fee's a wise woman. Did she suggest you tell me?"

"I learned that from my parents' experience. My mother waited until after she and my dad were married to let him know about her abilities. He didn't like it. He didn't like Fee either, my mother's sister witch, for years and years."

"He's sure changed his mind."

"Yes, he has."

Werner came around the table to sit in the chair beside me, his hands clasped so he wouldn't reach for me. "I suspected you were psychic, which is why I didn't want to know for sure where your information came from, though if you remember, I kept suggesting you had an edge."

I sat straighter. "Yes, I remember."

"I'm a bit psychic myself, though I've never admitted it to anyone, and I don't want anyone in Mystic to know, which shows how much I trust you. It could ruin my rep as a detective."

All I could think of was how psychic our children might be. Talk about premature.

He kissed his way from my wrist to my inner elbow, lips but no hands. "I think I've always known that you belong to me."

Great, so he echoes my thoughts. "We haven't exactly established that, yet."

"We will, as soon as you let me touch you. Any other secrets you care to share?"

"Don't you want to know what I've seen so far in the case we're working on?"

"All I want at this moment is to take that dress off you." He traced the leather at the lowest point of my plunging neckline, but he stroked nothing but fabric. Touching but not. Raising my expectations and shivering me to my Ferragamos.

With some bit of psychic communication, we stepped away from the table, and Werner swept me off my feet and carried me up the stairs to his room.

His bed had been transformed, covered as it was with wildly expensive bedding, the spread a cool Vera Bradley–type sea of paisley silk in cobalts and teals. Manly but sexy to the skin. When Werner threw back the comforter, he set me down on decadent electric-blue sheets. Real silk, not polyester fakes.

"I'm worried I might lose you in there," he said. "Your dress is the same color."

I silently opened my arms to him.

At three in the morning we nuked supper and ate from deep cereal bowls, sitting next to each other on the sofa, me wearing his shirt, my bare legs over his lap, again touching but not. When he picked up a meatball, I laughed the way I'd wanted to when he'd dropped the first, and he laughed with me.

The laughter made me think of my parents. Dad and Mom. Dad and Aunt Fee. And I reached for Werner again, so the food was forgotten.

I didn't get to the shop until noon the next day. Not smiling like a calf-eyed puppy was a chore.

To give Eve credit, she said nothing snarky and let me lead the conversation. "We have to go sleuthing tonight," I said.

"What about Werner?"

"He's got a day of meetings that won't end until after midnight, so I suggested he and I skip tonight. Make him wait."

"Shut! Up!"

I looked up from my perusal of the seventies formals.

"Little Wiener, you called him. So? Is he?"

I tried to look stern. Crossed my arms, firmed my lips, tapped a pointy-toed René Mancini sheer zip bootee, but I couldn't hold my laughter. "That was a pre-psychic call. Huge mistake. Huge!" I stressed.

"I knew it! You lucky—I miss Kyle."

I chuckled. "For tonight, you sleep at my house. We'll play some loud concert on TV that'll send Dad and Fiona to her house. Alex hasn't moved in yet, so we'll have the place to ourselves."

"You're an everything-turns-to-gold brat."

"Go tell my mother that. Listen, we've got to be ready to roll at midnight, and it'll be easier to leave an empty house."

"What do you two have your heads together over?" Dolly asked, coming into the area behind the back-walled checkout counter. Good thing she was deaf. "You look like you're up to no good," she said.

"You should know," I responded, and her cackle improved everybody's spirits, even Dante's—my spirit's spirits.

Eve shrugged as she put her father's army coat in the closet. "I can't believe Mad left the shop in the middle of the afternoon yesterday and stayed away for an entire twenty-four hours," she griped, laying it on to take them off the sleuthing scent, "just because she and Werner are a couple."

I couldn't help smiling or remembering the romance of our time together. "He is a charmer," I said, remembering our short but powerful night.

"Oh, barf," Eve said, watching me.

Dolly wagged a finger and gave her a "Tut tut tut. What's wrong with you, Eve Meyers? Have you lost all sense of romance? Where's that nice Kyle DeLong these days?"

"He's running the Parisian arm of DeLong Enterprises," Eve said on a sigh.

"We need to find you a man."

Eve grumped. "No offense, Dolly, but could you find me one about seventy-five years younger than you are?"

I thought Dolly would laugh up a lung. She had a charming laugh, if you weren't afraid she'd kill herself using it, but I still got a peek at the girl Dante had fallen for. Heck, I'd once worn the body of the girl Dante had fallen for. It was a scary but romantic minute, and I got out just in time. Dante showed himself now just to watch her. He had no concern for her health; she'd be his when her life ended. He stood, arms crossed, his grin pretty darned deadly. I could tell by the look on his face that it wouldn't be long before Dolly disappeared from our work area.

I hadn't thought about the case or the formal entries since yesterday, when I'd left to spend time with Lytton.

Problem was, I was dying to find out how the case was going, but we just hadn't found time to talk about it. "We need more hangers," I said. "I'll go get some."

When I got to my second-floor workroom, I speed-dialed Werner. "Hey, how did it go with the O'Dowds yesterday? Did you learn anything about Robin? I can't believe we didn't talk about this last night."

"If you want to talk anytime soon, we'll have to sit outside in a park where I can't ravish you."

I sighed, remembering.

"Truth is, as soon as I mentioned Wayne's dead sister, Wynona zipped it. I get to question them Friday morning at nine with their lawyer present."

"Darn. Anything else new? What about Bambi-Jo?"

"I thought I'd question her after I finished going through the boxes of info I got from the country club."

"Ooh, wish I could go through them with you. Can I come by after work?"

"No, because I've got a suspect coming in, and I don't want him to see you."

"What? Who?"

"Zavier McDowell."

"Oh, that's not fair. You wouldn't know him if he hadn't waved us down. Be nice to him. Life hasn't been."

"You told me you found out about him from an anonymous tip."

Maybe confessing my abilities had muddied the waters. Too late to worry about. "That was true. That wasn't a vision. I got a tip about the key and some vague person who might have hidden the stuff in a drainpipe. No names were given to me." Zavier was also probably the person who'd hidden the brass box in my attic, but I wanted to approach Zavier about that so he wouldn't be afraid.

"But was the tip anonymous?"

As anonymous as a ghost could get. "Absolutely."

"Our perp could as easily have been Zavier's brother, the councilman. We got a search warrant to search Bradenton Cove, especially Zavier's room, but we didn't find any of the scavenged items, not even the cane we saw him using."

I tried to defend Zavier. Something told me he wasn't guilty.

"He's prone to telling everything he knows, and his name's on the guest list for that night. Plus, he has a history of sexual harassment," Werner countered.

"Say what?"

"Three times. His family always made it go away. The victims all declined to press charges. He very well might have scared Robin into jumping in the ocean that night. I'm just bringing him in for questioning, Mad."

All the more reason why I had to step up my sleuthing. "I forgive you. You're simply doing your job."

"Thanks loads. I'm sorry I won't see you tonight."

"Thanks for yesterday. It was—"

"Incredible." He cleared his throat. "To set the record straight," he said, just short of a whisper, "I love sharing supper and breakfast with you, and I especially love our time in between."

"My knees are weak. Who would've thought, back in third grade?"

"The Wiener and the Glamazon? No way." I loved the smile in his voice as I hung up.

A bit dazed—doubly so, between the upper of remembering last night and the downer of learning about Zavier's background—I grabbed an armful of hangers and went back downstairs.

"Okay," I said, returning to the racks of formals. "Time to get back to work."

"Don't act like we're the slackers," Eve said. "You played hooky yesterday, and now, stalling tactics?"

I winked. "Jealous?"

My BFF stuck her tongue out at me.

"Girls, girls, you're both pretty," Aunt Fiona said, entering the room. "Cut the squabbling and get to work. We have a lot to do, and I'll be in panic mode until it's done."

I kissed her cheek and looked around. "Yes, ma'am. Okay, I already see a few bloopers. The Bob Mackies; there are three on the label rack, am I correct? Mackie designed for Cher in the seventies. He didn't start his label line until 1982. Pull them aside to be returned. They weren't worn to the country club's fiftieth, not unless somebody borrowed them from Judy Garland or Cher."

"My stars," Dolly said. "You do know your stuff, Madeira."

"Thank you, Dolly." I looked at the single formal I'd chosen. "Hang the peach crepe silk with the chevron-striped apron and tulle petticoats beside the airman's uniform." I was being forced to pick Vainglory's dress for a reading with her wearing it. Much more powerful. I hated to give Deborah VanCortland the satisfaction, but maybe I'd find a way to use the pair of antique shoe-shaped ink bottles her son and my sister gave me as a maid-of-honor gift to out her as being part of the scavenger hunt.

Dolly tittered, and she wasn't looking at us. "Oh, I think I need to go work in Paris when it Sizzles," she said, distracted.

My resident ghost, her former lover, must have appeared just beyond the counter wall and waved her his way.

I could have used Dolly's help, but at 106, the old girl deserved to have some fun.

"Go ahead, but while you're in there, pray that we find out who put that cash box in my attic and when. You hear me? It's important that I know the answer, and praying, no matter how loud, doesn't seem to be working for me. I can't seem to connect with the big guy, if you get my drift."

Dolly laughed a little hard for a private joke, but Eve didn't seem to think anything of it. Well, Dolly was Dolly.

My head came up at that. I sure hoped it wasn't Dolly who'd put the box in the attic. Oh, heck no. Forty years ago, she would have been in her late sixties and never would have been a member of that clique. Silly me. Which begged the obvious question: Why was Dante protecting Zavier?

"Look at this gown," Fiona said. "I think I have a picture of it."

The picture hadn't done Vainglory's dress justice. I knew that because I'd seen her take off her petticoat from beneath it and tear it into the pieces that would be used to hide the evidence.

"That's the one."

I wouldn't know, without a doubt, who the real owner was until the first fitting. Deborah might have sold it after Cort divorced her. I did hope, however, that it would be the same poor little rich girl. Thank the stars that Sherry's Kathleen and Riley would have Fiona as a second grandmother.

"Fiona, can you lift the skirt?"

She did.

"Darn, the petticoats are missing. There should be at least four, all made of tulle, and a crinoline."

Not to mention the torn petticoat which just might hold the key to a murder.

Twenty-four

O what a sight were Man, if his attires
Did alter with his minde;
And like a dolphins skinne, his clothes combin'd
With his desires!

—GEORGE HERBERT, 1593–1633

As I predicted, dad found it necessary to go and help Fiona with some handiwork—bad choice of words, Dad—around nine, the minute the rock concert started on television.

"We'll see you tomorrow," she mouthed before he dragged her out the door.

After they drove away, Eve and I high-fived each other and turned the blaring thing off. I checked my watch. "What say we get a few hours' sleep and plan to sneak down to the old docks around one?"

"Are we setting our alarms for midnight or one?" she asked, with her hand on the doorknob to Sherry's old room.

"Alarm for one, we'll be there by half past."

"Gotcha."

I thought about what I'd take for protection and decided the Taser gun, pepper spray, and a hammer would do, all of which were already in my Coach bag. But I needed a less expensive carryall for our foray into the world of greasy old mills.

Three and a half hours later, my alarm clock rang. Two seconds later, my door slammed open. "Ugh," Eve said.

"Yep." We were both still dressed. "I left the coffee on. Let's grab a cup and hit the road."

By one twenty, we had hit the mill section, where I hoped to find the warehouse/belly of the whale/whatever, where more clues were hidden in a makeshift pipe handrail and where I believed the scavenger hunters had gathered in the wee hours of the morning in question.

We left Eve's car and started with the farthest mill so we could work our way back to the car.

I flashed my light around the first. It had ceilings like a Vanderbilt mansion. "This sure isn't it."

We left and checked a second that looked more like a center walkway between two floors of offices. "Not this one, either." Though both of them were decrepit, neither had brick walls, inside or out.

The third was in the worst condition by far—read: skittering squealing rats with debris and dust at every step. The place frankly shivered me to my bones. I ran the flashlight along the inside walls as I'd done in the first two, and there it was, plain as day: The word "steam," barely visible on the disintegrating brick wall. I wouldn't have been able to read it, if I didn't already know what it said.

I turned toward the center of the room, but there was no more stairway. Gone, except for the top step hanging in the air off the floor above, a floor that could probably fall on our heads any minute.

Beneath the former stairs, scattered on the ground and across the room, I spotted the kind of fat plumbing pipes I remembered and sought now, some still jointed, some not.

"We have to look inside pipes like that." I circled a group with my flashlight. "Start with the ones on the floor around where the stairway used to be."

Eve gave a whole-body shiver with an accompanying whine of a sound, like something evil had just passed through her. "You jest."

"'Fraid not."

"Where the stairway *used* to be. I wasn't in your vision."

I flashed my light in a circle beneath the opening in the ceiling.

"Oh," she said.

I flashed my light into open-ended pipes first.

Mice skittered around us, all cautious-like, until Eve screamed and screamed some more and threw a pipe against a wall, which caused brick dust to rain around the periphery of the room . . . and all the rodents to disappear.

I clamped one hand over her mouth and the other around her throwing arm. "Way to bring the police, Meyers," I whispered near her ear.

Above my hand, her eyes were wider than dinner plates. Okay, I'm exaggerating. "Can you shut up now?" I asked. "No more throwing?"

A nod. The circumference of her eyes narrowed to the proportions of a saucer, yet still worthy of the *Guinness Book of World Records*.

"Rats!" she snapped.

I nudged her arm. "You expected good housekeeping and a hot toddy?"

She huffed. Then she did a little boot-scootin'. "To keep them away," she said.

I sighed. "Forgot to specify: Be quiet. Wish I had a camera, though. You had that tantrum because of a rat in a pipe?"

"No, that pipe had a whole tenement thing going on. They multiply like poor families in walk-ups during the Depression. At least three families and sixteen pink erasers shared one hovel."

"Pink erasers?"

"Newborn ratlets."

I snorted. "Scarred for life, are you?"

"Yes, you major pain in the butt seam."

"Sorry. Here, check this pipe."

She emitted a toned-down squeal. But she accepted it, placed it on a three-legged table, took a racehorse-at-the-gate pose, and shined her flashlight inside.

Her release of breath and recovered stance said it was empty.

"There's something in it," she said. "Just there, wrapped in something, I think."

I flashed my own light in there. "I definitely see filthy pink in two places." My first inclination was to bang the pipe against the floor to dislodge whatever was at the top end of the pipe, the T joint end. But I worried about noise and possible breakage, so I figured I'd get it out at home, or in the shop when I was alone, so I slipped the fat pipe in my liquor store bag I'd brought instead of my Coach bag.

Eve gasped and started dragging me away.

"Wait," I said.

"No, someone's coming," she whispered.

I heard voices in the distance. More than one. An argument in whispers. A man and a woman, maybe. Hard to tell with whispers. Could be two of either. Or more of a gang.

I smelled chocolate, and I knew I should follow the scent.

I grabbed Eve's arm and turned her. She came and sniffed, and we jogged toward the scent, ending up in a closet with the half door hanging by a hinge. We could just barely still hear them.

"This is stupid," one whispered.

"Take it out of the stair rails," someone different whispered. "You know where you put it. The police are nosing around. Throw it in the drink."

So one of the people had to be Tuxman, the guy whose voice I hadn't recognized the night he hid his loot in the stair-rail pipe.

"We could have done this in the morning," Tuxman replied.

"And risk being seen?" The second speaker's voice made me think of the man/woman/mechanical-voice caller Dolly had spoken to.

In our hiding spot, the chocolate scent drew us down low, beneath a lower shelf, where a piece of outside wall was missing. Getting out meant bellying our way through slowly, in perfect silence, but we did.

It seemed to take forever.

I didn't recognize the dock we came out on, but I did recognize the name of the fishing boat ten feet away. The *Yacht C*.

"Is anybody here?" We heard Tuxman call.

I pulled Eve along, onto the boat and out of sight. We looked around, but it was empty. "In my second vision," I said, "I heard the *Yacht C* named as a hiding place."

"Your visions are starting to tick me off," Eve said.

"You take lookout, make sure those thugs aren't coming here to look for more of the hidden items they scavenged. I'll look to see if I can find more of the missing items."

Eve shrugged.

"At least it'll keep us busy until it's safe to go back to your car."

"Why is it always my car, I'd like to know?"

"Because mine has the name of my shop on it."

"How bloody convenient."

Noise continued coming from the warehouse, so we couldn't leave. I found no hidden treasure but a bunk that I chose not to examine too closely.

Eve came to join me. "I just heard a car. I think they're leaving but we should wait awhile to make sure."

"Good thinking." We sat, straight up. Eventually, we leaned against each other, waiting until we would feel safe to go home.

Raucous laughter came from nowhere and had us sitting at attention again. Noise and movement. Salty language. Three or more men.

The moon shone on my watch. Four in the morning.

Eve slapped my arm back and forth. "They're going fishing!" she whispered as the motor started.

"Zeke, bring the supplies below," a man said.

"Yes, Cap'n."

We scrambled, found something like a trapdoor, and

ended up in a stinking but empty tank-like area, where we huddled in a corner, with Eve dry heaving and me trying not to join her. Fortunately the motor drowned her out.

Eventually we must have gotten used to the smell, because suddenly daylight was hitting us in the face.

"Ah, daylight," Eve said, but her joy was short-lived, as the hold then filled with crushed ice and squirming, jumping, stinking fish of all kinds, some with legs.

We stood and screamed, but nobody heard us.

A rogue lobster, a granddaddy, grabbed at my hair, and ended up with a claw full. A crab looked Eve right in the eye.

She slapped it away with a fish. "They're dying, you know."

"What?"

"They're not in the water anymore. They're dying around us."

We screamed our throats raw, and when the fish stopped sailing in, everything went quiet.

Our rescuers did not take kindly to our presence on the trawler. As a matter of fact, "salty" became a mild description of their reaction. The blankets they gave us did not help warm us. Not only didn't they get us out of there fast, they intended to wait till they got their quota for the day. They even called the police on us.

"How rude," Eve whispered for my ears only.

"Tell the Mystick Falls police that it's Maddie Cutler," I said.

The captain did as I asked. Then it was, "Yes, Detective," and "No, Detective."

He hung up. "There's a missing persons bulletin out on you two."

"At least somebody missed us," Eve said.

"Not until they found your car near a murder scene."

Twenty-five

My wife dresses to kill. She cooks the same way.
—HENNY YOUNGMAN

The dock showers reminded me of a tenter's campground—rough, damp wood—but the captain insisted, and the generous spray worked three ways: stench removal, revival, and warmth. Even the generic soap smelled like a bouquet of wildflowers. Frankly, we went in stinking enough to pass the high mark on the barf-o-meter.

When I finished, though I never wanted to step from the steaming heat of that water, I peeked around the shower curtain and found that my clothes had been replaced with a navy jumpsuit and a gunmetal gray towel, both clean, but rough enough to sand a boat deck. Evidently, fishermen do not believe in fabric softener.

The jumpsuit's fish-shaped patch proclaimed me a member of the boat's crew. "Zeke," as it happened, was embroidered beneath the larger *Yacht C* on the patch.

When I opened the door to my shower cubby, I came face-to-face with Gus, aka Eve, my BFF.

"Boy, these suits are rough," I said. "They abrade the nips something fierce, don'tcha think?" I turned to leave the showers, and came face-to-face with Werner.

He kissed me senseless, being careful not to abrade the nips further, the dear. When he stepped away, it took him a minute to compose himself. "Just when I think I want to beat you," he said, "you make me want to make love to you."

"What changed your mind?" Eve asked. "Not that I'm not glad."

"I heard about you being covered in fish."

"So, we amuse you?" I said, getting some extra mileage off the warmth filling me over his tender care and his thermonuclear kiss.

"You infuriate me!" he thundered.

"Sheesh, you nearly knocked us back to the showers with the force of that roar."

"After two hours of sleep—"

"Speaking of last night, how'd it go at the country club?"

"They had their lawyers, plural, what do you think? I had to request a subpoena to get those pictures and one to search the club, though I'm most interested in the basement. But don't think you distracted me from my tirade, Minx."

I tried to look innocent as I plucked the sandpaper fabric away from my sore nips.

Eve snickered.

Werner swallowed. "Two hours' sleep, like I said, and I'm called out of bed because Eve's car's been found at a murder scene. I cringed with every corner I turned in those rat-hole mill buildings, afraid I was gonna find one or both of you with nooses around your pretty little necks. The very necks I so often want to close my hands around. Except that one of them now means more to me than my own skin. Something like that sobers a man."

I shivered, from cold and relief. "You're sending mixed signals, Detective."

He growled.

I stepped back. "So," I said, trying to keep from placing a hand on my hip. This was no time to poke the tiger. "You were worried about us."

"You scared the living tar out of me!"

"I calculate that as another seven-point-nine shout on the Richter," I said, though my voice had trailed off at his warning look.

Werner gave me the evil eye while he handed Eve his cell phone. "Call your mother, then let Mad call her dad."

I stamped a foot. "You told them we were missing?"

"Don't start with the accusations, because I can trump you, baby."

He so could.

"I, unfortunately, believed that someone stole your car, Eve, and the two of you were home safe. But to answer your question, Madeira, in proving that fact to myself, I inadvertently told your parents you were missing."

"How long ago was that?" I began calculating my father's stress level. "I mean, how long have you been look-ing for us?" I asked while Eve calmed her mother.

"Eve's car was called in as abandoned around two, the patrolmen took a look around, found the dead body, and now it's ten in the morning."

I raised a wait-a-minute finger and dialed Fiona's house. She picked up, sobbed when she heard my voice, then my dad was shouting at me, making threats that gave me the warm fuzzies. He loved me, he said with all the wrong words. What got to me was his voice cracking during the disjointed tirade. "I love you, too, Daddy. Fiona, too."

"Don't let them come down here," Werner said. "It's a zoo."

"Wait there for me. Be home soon," I said. "Our house, okay?"

I gave Werner his phone back, and because I didn't want an emotional response to become Werner's reason that I should stop sleuthing, I ran with the crime. "What did they find? Who got murdered? How? When? Where? Why?"

Werner slipped his phone onto his belt clip and looked up. "You really should get a job on the force."

"Thank you."

"Not a compliment. That was a nice way of saying 'Stop freaking sleuthing!'"

"I'll try," I said, in the same way a kid says they'll try eating peas. It's so far off, you can be truthful about trying, sort of. "Who got murdered?"

Werner cupped his neck, indicating that I was, to him, a lost cause, but his eyes said different. "We're not sure yet," he said, "whether to call the death a murder or suicide. Forensics will have to step in. The victim left what looks like a suicide note."

A murder staged as a suicide, I said to myself, remembering the voices we'd run from.

"You know that besides your fishing boat, there's a luxury yacht also called the *Yacht Sea*," Werner said, changing the subject. "Which makes your little jaunt of last night a bit fishy. Visionary info?"

Eve huffed. "You told him?"

Werner eyed her until she shivered. Then she straightened. "Detective, we heard voices, so we ran," she said. "The boat looked like the best hiding place. The only hiding place. We figured we'd give it time, and we fell 'asleep. Next thing, the crew's onboard and talking about stowing something below, so we duck into the hold."

I shrugged and nodded. "You know the rest."

Werner looked from one of us to the other. "We will, in future, discuss your antics of this night in depth," he said.

Not if I could distract him. "Go on," I said as we reached his car. "Where did you find the victim? I need names, details."

"We found him on the floor beside a broken ceiling beam attached to a chunk of ceiling with a noose around his neck. Preliminary exam shows that he died before the noose was slipped around his neck."

He? I shivered. "How'd he die?"

"Blunt force trauma to the head."

"It would have taken someone strong to lift a dead weight and slip a noose around it," I said. "And you haven't told us who it was or what the suicide note said."

"Wayne O'Dowd died in that brick hellhole tonight, a printed confession clenched in his cold, dead hand."

"That's suspicious," I said.

"It's printed with his printer. Here's something equally suspicious. On his computer screen at home is a blog entry. He was the Mystick Falls Masque."

"Ohhh," I said. "Trying to get justice for his sister's death. That makes so much sense."

"You would think so, but the note said *he* took his sister, Robin, out on the *Yacht Sea* and threw her overboard for her inheritance."

I gasped. "That note lies!"

"I personally think so, too, and we don't know if Wayne or his murderer wrote his last blog entry, but it said the investigation was at an end. The Phantom Masque signed it 'Over and out.'"

"Dead out," Eve said.

Twenty-six

Today, fashion is really about sensuality—how a woman feels on the inside. In the '80s women used suits with exaggerated shoulders and waists to make a strong impression. Women are now more comfortable with themselves and their bodies—they no longer feel the need to hide behind their clothes.
—DONNA KARAN

We drove in silence for a bit, my mind running a marathon, Werner sitting beside me in the backseat, Eve up front with Billings. "Detective," I said, "who on the old police report is recorded as having said they were with Robin when the rogue wave took her?" I asked. "Who's telling the truth? Any of them, or not even the suicide note?"

"My guess is, none of them." He handed me the rolled-up morning paper from his pocket.

I opened it and gasped: "Zavier McDowell arrested for 1973 death of Robin O'Dowd."

"You arrested Zavier?"

"He confessed, Mad."

"Why didn't you call me?"

"I wanted to, for all the wrong reasons, but I was up to

my neck in paperwork until the call on Eve's car came in. Then we found a dead body in the same vicinity, which made finding you two my top priority." He grabbed me around the neck and pulled me against him, his kiss a testament to his worry. I reveled in it and gave as good as I got.

At a light, Eve fake gagged. "Cut it out!"

"I thought you hated Nick, not Werner."

"Nick left you too often. Werner demonstrates his affection too often."

"You're jealous," I said on a chuckle.

I nearly pulled away from Werner's hold, until I realized he'd been more than a little worried; more anxious than any detective should be when searching for a possible second body.

"I don't know who leaked Zavier's confession to the press," Werner said, finally letting go, "but Councilman McDowell and his lawyer were there, and they brought a couple of doctors and his live-in nurse to say Zavier couldn't have done it. Then the poor man ups and says he did."

I read the short article, zeroing in on pertinent details. "'Robin O'Dowd's 1973 death was reopened this week in the wake of newly unearthed evidence . . . No additional details provided . . . Detective Lytton Werner declined comment' . . . yada yada yada. 'Anyone with information about the case is being asked to contact the Mystick Falls Police Department.'"

"It's nothing but a puff piece," Werner said.

"Enough to do Zavier some damage," I said. "Tell me he's not in jail."

"Right now he's refusing bail."

My head came up. "Well, there's got to be a story there, but at least he's safe." I released a breath. "Now, with Wayne's confession, we have *two* killers?"

"And two deaths," Eve said. "But one solved."

"If we believe Wayne's confession," I added.

"As I see it, we're back where we started," Werner said. "Robin O'Dowd's death is as much of a mystery as ever. The confessions cancel each other out, along with the original conclusion. Hey, what were you two doing down at the docks? That car wasn't parked anywhere near the *Yacht C.*"

Eve squeaked, the brat, at about the same time her mother and my parents flew out my father's front door.

I was smothered in hugs and love, all of us swallowing convulsively. I had been scared, both at the mill and on the boat last night, plus my nips were practically raw from wearing a sandpaper suit without a bra. And every hug made it worse.

Aunt Fee threw her arms around Werner. His stern expression dissolved as he looked at me over her shoulder, almost calf-eyed. He stepped from Fee's embrace and hugged my shoulder, pulling me against his like a big brother, but I melted into his arms.

For half a beat, he held me like I was his, until his eyes met my dad's, and he offered my father his hand. "Sir, may I have your permission to love your daughter?"

Had Werner's voice cracked? Who knew? At my dad's stupefied nod, he kissed me quick and hard, got in the patrol car, and Billings drove him away.

That started everyone on a string of questions.

"Aunt Fee, can you get me a paper bag to hold the contents of this stinky bag so I can throw it away out here?"

"I'll do it," Aunt Fee said. "You two run up and take a shower."

Eve hesitated. "Mom?"

"She's staying until you're warm and dressed in your own clothes," Aunt Fee said, and Mrs. Meyers nodded and took Eve's hand to go inside.

The two of us ran up to take our respective showers. I felt like nothing would erase the fish smell. I chose my most strongly scented hair products, soaps, and creams and blew my nose about ten times, then I found the silkiest padded bra I could find—after I'd moisturized.

When I got into my room, Aunt Fiona had transferred the makeshift weapons and wrapped treasures from the stinky liquor bag I left outside into a reusable grocery bag. "I won't even ask," she said, opening her arms to me.

Stupid me. When I stepped into her embrace, I burst into tears.

"Mom came to our rescue," I confessed. "We followed the scent of chocolate to safety."

"Don't tell your father you had such a close call."

"I know. Thanks for being here so I can tell you."

"Get dressed and come down. Brunch is waiting. Mrs. Meyers and I went a bit overboard, and your father needs a good long hug himself. And we want to know when you admitted to yourself that you're in love with Detective Werner. We've known for ages." She touched the piece of drainpipe on my nightstand, shook her head, and left.

Funny thing happened when I picked up the drainpipe I'd stolen from Bradenton Cove to put it away before anyone else saw it: I noticed that it seemed weighted. I mean, I held it at one end, and the opposite end fell, like it was heavier. I balanced it with my hands a distance apart and saw I was right.

Werner had held it by only one end, probably the heavy end, and had uncapped it that way, at the light end.

Determined to discover the weight discrepancy, I used the claws of the hammer in the grocery bag, one of my weapons of choice for the evening, to uncap the heavy end. No easy feat, but I did it. Then I put on a pair of gloves to handle whatever I found inside.

Nothing fell out of the uncapped end, but I flashed a light inside and it was packed so tight, it wouldn't have jiggled for anyone. It certainly didn't budge for me.

I tugged on the wrapping, and it tore. Tissue paper. I tore at that paper until I got the first piece out. A gold locket with a letter R on it, with a picture of a man and woman inside. Rather damning evidence, considering. Next, I pried out a man's ring with a brick of a diamond in it, five carats, maybe. I checked the inside of the band. No initials, but 24K. Next I found an emerald art deco pendant that my mother would have adored, a purse-size Lalique perfume bottle, probably worth a fortune because of its size. Last, an antique pocket watch with all kinds of compartments and dials. If Zavier had scavenged all this, he'd been right, he might have won, if . . . Robin had cooperated?

Speculation, I told myself. Nothing more. Besides, Zavier's brother, Councilman Eric McDowell, had also been there. He could as easily have hidden these pieces with their Day's—read Dad's—cars.

I put everything in a bottom drawer for later, when I'd

have a chance to dig inside the stair pipe Eve had found, and if I found more treasure there, I'd give it all to Werner at the same time.

He now knew about my psychometric gift. Heck, he now knew all the intimate little details about me.

The couple that sleuths together, stays together. Or not?

Twenty-seven

> The most reliable thing in my closet [is] my old RAF military jacket bought years ago at Portobello Market in my old neighborhood in Notting Hill, London. It looks great with jeans, leather pants, or even a cocktail dress. Plus I love the history of it.
> —PADMA LAKSHMI

My first fitting for *This Is Your Life* had been scheduled for the next morning.

"Mr. Jay Gilchrist?" I asked when he stepped into the shop, much too young to have worn the airman's uniform to the country club's fiftieth.

The man who saluted wore stonewashed jeans, a scruffy pair of regulation gunboots, and a high-quality camouflage T-shirt.

I saluted back. "At ease."

"Sorry," he said. "Habit, when my name is called."

I led him toward the dressing room. "I'm glad there are no half-dressed women in and out of the stalls."

"Yes, ma'am. I guess you don't get too many men in here."

"More than you think. I suppose I should have had separate dressing rooms built, but I do have a bathroom. Men

193

usually try things on in there. Except that I need the riser and the three-way mirrors to do a fitting. Are you in the service, too?"

"Yes, ma'am. I'm a lifer. Surprised you can tell."

"It's your stance. Very military."

"Glad I can go to this event, like my parents did. Curious to see what they're going to find out about my life. The pickin's will be pretty slim. I wouldn't be having this fitting if I wasn't chosen for the *This Is Your Life* segment, right?"

"That's right." I handed him the uniform on its hanger. "Go put it on, then stand on the platform in front of the mirrors there, so I can make sure it fits."

"I don't expect it will," he said, walking away.

I didn't think so either. "Yell when you're ready."

"Yes, ma'am."

"I'm ready," he said a short while later.

He looked beautiful, though a bit like he was playing dress-up. "My first reaction," I said, watching him come toward me, "is that you lost weight, except that you need more room in the shoulders, less in the waist, and I'd think you grew a half inch or so taller."

"These were my daddy's. I never met him. I don't know anything about him except his name. I'm hoping to learn about him when they talk about my life. It's pretty tame other than . . . you know, the war, and all that."

"Do you have a picture of your father wearing this to the fiftieth?"

"Yes, ma'am. Here it is." Jay handed it to me. It was framed. "That's him. You can tell he's looking at somebody he loves," Jay said.

"Can I keep this?"

"No, it's all I have of him."

"May I make a copy of it for the *This Is Your Life* segment? I think they're going to enlarge and display them."

"Sure. You can make a copy."

"Good. You fill out this form so I can call you when the uniform has been altered, and I'll run upstairs to use the copy machine." I had to take the picture out of the frame to scan it. I looked for a name in gold leaf at the bottom, or at least on the back, but this picture had been backed by black felt paper.

I returned as quickly as I could. "Here you go," I said, handing it back to him in the fitting room. Then I knelt to start fitting Jay's father's aged blue-gray uniform to him. "He was a handsome man, your dad. You take after him in looks."

Jay colored a bit at the backdoor compliment.

"You don't say much, do you?" I asked.

"No ma'am. I've learned to speak when spoken to."

I chuckled. "I'm having trouble filling in the conversation by myself."

"On the form," he said, "I didn't leave a phone number. I'll call you. Every day if you want. Just tell me when."

"You live in Rhode Island, I see."

"Scituate. My grandma's place."

"And your dad?"

Jay tilted his head.

I shut up, looked down, and kept pinning. I'd recently discovered that if I bought extra-long common pins with big round heads, I could carefully pin a garment without touching the fabric. I held the pin just so and let it do the touching. It took a while to devise the technique but I had aced it, unless I got distracted.

"Heard through a military grapevine when I was a kid that my dad was a prisoner of war until he went missing."

"I'm sorry to hear that."

A controlled shrug. "I never gave up looking. I've got this sense he's out there, wanting to find me as badly as I want to find him."

"Are you just a little bit psychic, maybe?"

"My grandma says I'm intuitive, like her. Since I got the call that I was coming here, my stomach has been flipping and cheering. It's like I've got corn popping in there."

"Because you're so excited to be on *This Is Your Life*?"

"Don't think I'm crazy, but it has to do with meeting you. I think that's why I'm talking so much."

"You're hardly talking at all, but never mind that. Keep going."

"I don't know but I have this feeling that there's a connection between you and my past."

"It's actually my parents who are chairing the *This Is Your Life* segment of the ball. I'm only judging and altering the vintage formals."

Jay shrugged. "There's something about you. I can't put my finger on it. I've been reading that blog. It's not your parents helping that detective. It's you. I know my dad is a piece of that puzzle somehow, and I'm counting on you to find the key."

I sat back on my legs, rather shaken, and looked up at him. "That's a tall order, soldier."

"I think you're up to it. I believe in you."

Dante appeared in the corner of the dressing room, a distance behind Jay. I tried not to react. "Ask him his father's name," he suggested.

"Jay, turn so I can see how the uniform fits in the back."

I was trying not to react to Dante, so it would be easier if my intuitive model couldn't see my face. "Tell me, Jay, what's your father's name?"

"Glen Gilchrist."

"Gilchrist. I can see a family resemblance, if it's the same family," Dante said. "I think Dolly and I went to school with his . . . *great*-grandfather, name of Liam. He would probably have been this boy's paternal grandmother's father. Liam knew things, too. Had the sense when something momentous was about to happen. Kids made fun of him, but trust this boy's intuition. Maybe Werner can help you try to find his father."

Jay cleared his throat. "Why do I feel as if something is happening, even in the silence of the moment?"

"Must be the smell of burning rubber. I'm thinking."

Jay chuckled.

"Turn," I said.

He nearly saluted as he obeyed.

"You look born to the uniform, and you'll look even better when I'm done with you."

"Thank you, ma'am. I'm in the same branch of the service, and, every chance I get, I pester anybody who might be able to help find my dad, from general to clerk, anybody who can get their hands on classified information."

My heart sped, and I tried not to let my eyes fill. This man had lost his father to his country, and his tenacity touched me deeply. I picked up the picture of his dad. "Well, you look just like him. Have you tried posting the picture online?"

"Ma'am, I've tried everything, every way, all the way up to and through the secretary of defense. He is listed as MIA."

"My condolences."

"I don't accept them, and I apologize for being flip. But he's not dead."

"I respect and believe you." I looked up from my measuring tape and focused on him. "How did you get his uniform, if he didn't come back?"

Jay cleared his throat. "He left it behind. Nobody seems to know why, though it's been like a living connection that kept me searching. In a torn pocket, I found a letter addressed to no one but signed by him from the early days and it's filled with love."

"As if you were meant to have that love."

"Yes, ma'am."

"You know, we're about the same age. I wish you'd call me Maddie or Madeira."

"My training is strong. Not sure I can."

"I sort of knew that before I made the offer, but you're welcome to."

"You a bit psychic, too, ma'am?"

Funny he should ask as I intentionally touched the fabric, let my hand rest against the jacket's hem for a minute, allowing a familiar miasma to overtake me. For Jay's sake, given my bold and impetuous move, I found myself glad I was already kneeling on the floor. What would the poor boy think when I zoned? Or would a psychically sensitive person recognize what was happening?

I floated fast away from the real world, from my shop and the walls that surrounded me. I traveled like never before, as if on a wave. I felt water sluicing over me, raining down on me like the wrath of the gods, and in time, I felt buoyed and hopeful.

I took to floating, warming, because my man was carrying me from the cold shower, warming me as we went.

I, Madeira Cutler, had never had this experience in a vision before. Inside the body of another, a woman profoundly in love—physically, emotionally, spiritually—and judging by the eyes that looked into mine, my love was deeply returned. I got placed naked on a bed and got wrapped in the spread, then a blanket floated over me, tucked from the outside to beneath me, so I felt like a mummy.

Sweet words and soft kisses met my face. He toweled my hair. Warmth piled on warmth. He'd trapped me in a cocoon, until finally, a dear uniform jacket covered me from the shoulders down, above all the rest.

I touched the fabric to my nose, and inhaled his Old Spice scent. I released an arm, slipped a hand in his jacket pocket, and closed it around something odd, forged of metal and fabric.

"Let me in," my new husband said, distracting me, "I'll warm you with my body."

I hid, yet wallowed, deep inside her soul, though I could feel myself fading, but I stayed long enough to join her in lifting her blankets and his jacket, and opening our arms and heart, we let him in.

But as good as he felt, I floated away from him, from them, thank the universe, and I looked up at a concerned military man—the product of that love?—with a cup of water in his hand, and my head on his lap.

Twenty-eight

The intoxication obtained from wearing certain articles of
clothing can be as powerful as that induced by a drug.
                                        —BERNARD RUDOFSKY,
                        THE UNFASHIONABLE HUMAN BODY

I looked down at myself and found that Jay had covered
me with his jacket. His father's jacket, in the same way
that his father had covered his mother with it, hence my
vision.

I accepted the water he offered me and sipped it. "I forgot to eat breakfast, and it's past lunch."

"Here," he said. "Power bar." He unwrapped it and put
it in my hand.

I accepted with a nod and took a bite. "Mm. Strawberry.
Good. You never said anything about your mother."

He firmed his lips. "I lost her, too, but I always know
where to find her. Granite's granite after all."

A headstone. I hadn't sensed him mourning her death.

He helped me stand and kept an arm around my waist
until I took a seat on my mother's fainting couch in my sitting area. He sat in a chair facing me. "Do you have a date

for the Very Vintage Valentine dance at the country club?" he asked, shy for a military man.

"I do, yes."

"Oh. Too bad. I'm planning on being nervous," he said.

"You fight with guns for a living, and you think you'll have stage fright?"

"Humor me."

As far as I was concerned I was in a committed relationship. I was not sure Werner had reached that conclusion yet, though he sure gave new meaning to thermonuclear . . . everything.

"Why are you grinning?" Jay asked.

"New relationship. Detective Lytton Werner of the Mystick Falls Police Department. My last relationship ended about six months ago, with an FBI agent, a long-time friend. They both are, actually. School chums, the both of them."

"You favor powerful men. I'm sorry you won't be on my arm."

"I have two choices for you. I'd love to walk in with a man on each arm." I paused and hooked my left arm for him to take, and he nearly did.

"Hey, Mad," Eve said, coming in the front door, out of our line of sight from the dressing room.

"Or you can escort my best friend, Eve."

She stepped into the dressing room wearing a copper bustier with a calf-length pencil skirt of black lace over shiny copper. Her Little Shoe Box booties from 1996 were black patent leather pumps with four-inch heels and ankle straps with copper locks on them. One could also call her hair copper with black and blonde highlights.

I think Jay swallowed his tongue.

"I'm not a dom," Eve said, "like these shoes would imply. Just a goth with a steampunk edge and a BFF who can dress me properly. Mad, can I have an introduction?"

"Airman Jay Gilchrist, meet Eve Meyers, my best friend since third grade."

"Ms. Meyers," he said, forgetting I was in the room. "May I escort you to the Very Vintage Valentine ball at the country club? I won a spot as a *This Is Your Life*r."

"Mad has good taste. You surely deserve to have won a spot. I'd love to walk in on your arm, Airman."

The man's green-eyed grin just about stole my breath, so it was no surprise to me that Eve actually grabbed me to keep from losing her sea legs.

"I won't disappoint you," the airman said. "Can we sit with Madeira and her detective?"

"As long as you walk in on my arm," Eve said, "I don't care where we sit, but I would have sat with them if I was alone, so, perfect."

"It's a date," the airman said, tweaking her chin, tinkling a tiny bell of a button at her neck, and looking at me to find out our next move.

"You're all pinned up for alterations. You can go and change back into your own clothes."

When he shut the bathroom door, Eve erupted in squeals. "You found me the perfect man."

"You've only known him five minutes."

"He acts like I'm normal, which I am."

I regarded her from spiked copper hair to padlock-trimmed pumps. "Yep, normal. That uniform was his father's." I lowered my voice. "That uniform was his father's but he has one of his own. He'll ship out again and leave you behind. You ready for that?"

"He looks like he could be worth waiting for. We don't have to get engaged, right? The ball will only be our first date."

"Right."

"All things in their own time," Eve said without snark.

When Airman Gilchrist came out, he asked Eve to lunch, and even offered to bring me something. I declined and watched them leave the shop with a really good feeling about them in my gut and the knowledge that in a couple of days, that ball could be, like, their fifth date. "Jay, call me so I can tell you when the alterations are done," I shouted after him.

Then I locked the shop and called Werner, opening the picture of Airman Gilchrist's father. "Do you have the pictures of the people who attended the fiftieth as a result of your search warrant?"

"Yes, Madeira—you are not my boss—I do."

"Meet me here. I'll lock the shop for an hour. Late lunch/booty call/photo hunt. You choose the order. Bring a snack, though, besides yourself, I mean."

His phone went static, then dead.

Dante appeared, laughing. "Booty call? Here? Really? Where I can watch?"

I could have drowned in Dante's killer grin. I wagged a finger at him. "Now you show! Get lost."

"But you wanted answers."

"Now? Well, okay. Talk fast."

Dante leaned against my counter, arms crossed. "Zavier is innocent. Always will be."

"I believe that. But Werner said he confessed."

My ghost straightened. "He's protecting somebody he

loves or acting under orders from somebody who scares him to death. I saw him hide the box. He was crying like the boy he mentally is."

That broke my heart. "Point taken." I bit my lip, upset that an innocent like Zavier had to endure any of this.

"Who died that night at the warehouse?" Dante asked. "I heard just enough to know somebody did."

"Wayne O'Dowd. His wife is Wynona. She was in my vision but not him."

"Oh, he was there. He was a regular ringleader at those events. Could you identify everyone in your vision?"

"No, there's still the guy I dubbed Snake, and another I called Tuxman to keep them straight in my mind."

"Both could be Wayne. Oily. Everybody hated him. Slimy bastard."

"Wynona must be our first suspect." My head came up. "Hey, I forgot to tell Werner about you. That I could see and talk to ghosts. That you live with me here."

"You told him everything else? Visions, witchy tendencies?"

I nodded.

"Save me for Valentine's Day." He chuckled. "Back to Wynona."

"They called her Lady Backroom," I said.

Dante nodded. "She gets her husband's money, but Lady Backroom or not, she's not stupid enough to kill for it in the middle of a reopened investigation. After the fiftieth, she and hubby both wore guilt like diamonds. Dolly said that."

"What are we missing, then? Who wanted Wayne and Robin dead?"

"Wynona is too easy to fall back on for both murders, and somebody knew she would be. Don't overlook Zavier's family. He didn't fit the mold. He was a flaw in their perfect bloodline."

"Where's his mother?"

"Died while he was in the birth canal. He was deprived of oxygen too long."

"Fifty years ago, that kind of thing happened."

"Concentrate on his living family, Mad."

"Eric, I know. Councilman McDowell. I still hate that guy, but he wants to save Zavier from their father, and I don't know why. So now I have only a weakening dislike, because he seems to care what happens to his brother."

"For the McDowells," Dante said, "life is a stage and nothing is as it appears. And don't discount the father. Power is to Thatcher McDowell like blood is to vampires."

"Vampires? What the scrap do you know about vamps?"

"A vamp used to be a seductress in my day. But hey, you put a television upstairs for when you're sewing. I've been catching up on the world. And frankly, it's gotten scary. Not my fault you like Buffy reruns."

I chuckled, imagining his reactions. "Okay, I'll check out Zavier and Eric's father, Thatcher the vampire, the Savile Row suit wearer who snowed us at the country club," I said. "Oh, here comes Werner."

Dante faded. "I'll be upstairs," my ghost whispered, "wearing earphones—sort of."

I laughed nervously as the ghostly image departed and my hunky detective silently backed me to the fainting couch, his bedroom eyes boring into mine like a fast flash of pure seduction. When I hit the couch, I was forced to sit, while my hands trembled and my heart tripped a rapid beat. Then Werner gently pushed my shoulders back as he leaned over me. "Just a kiss to get us through the day."

I'm surprised the fainting couch didn't burst into flames. Just our hands touched, then our lips, for a thermonuclear kiss so hot, I wondered why we weren't radioactive.

I gasped for breath. "Where did you learn to kiss like that?" I asked. "I never—"

"Really? Never?" He crowed like an alpha cock in a henhouse.

"Where?" I repeated.

"Jocks are sought after in college and I was one of the best. It's called practice."

"It's called technique, like freezing your prey with a look. One kiss and you lure the sense right out of me. I'm like a jellyfish with the palsied tremblies panting for more."

"And after making love?" he asked.

"We both pass out. You're on an ego trip, aren't you?"

"You said I was better than . . . you know. Let me wallow, will you? I'll return to earth, or maybe not, because I want to kiss you again."

Someone started hammering on my door with a fist.

"Madeira Cutler, you let me in. I'm supposed to have a fitting in half an hour, and I need to start early so I can leave early. I have an important appointment. You can eat lunch later."

I sighed. "My sign says out to lunch, but my car's in the lot."

"So's mine." Werner furrowed his brows at the sound of her voice. "Tell me that's not—?"

"Yep. Deborah VanCortland in the flesh."

"You picked her for *This Is Your Life*? You have an exasperation wish?"

"I have visions. The petticoat pieces come from her petticoat. This way Dad and Aunt Fee will research the story of her life, plus I get to read the dress with her in it, always a more powerful read."

"Okay, when you put it that way, your visions make me worry about you. How much trouble can you get into in somebody else's body?"

I thought about the living Dante laying me on the bed while I occupied Dolly's body once, though I got out in time. I remembered the moment I stood on a high level of the Eiffel Tower with a gun pointed my way. "Nothing I can't escape."

"I've pulled you out of a few deep holes. Were those the results of visions?"

"No, just bad timing. I guess you need to see for yourself. We're sharing right now, so stay, but don't let on when I zone, and don't freak if I talk in someone else's voice."

"That's not funny, Madeira. And you may just be sharing, but I'm looking at us as having a committed relationship."

I threw my arms around him, reveling in his busy hands. "Me, too. Committed. A relationship. Yes!"

The banging on the door did not stop. We gave up. I went into my bathroom to freshen up while Werner straightened his jacket and tie and let Vainglory in.

I took one look at her when I came out and knew she hadn't changed a bit. Not since she'd stolen her mother's gown for the fiftieth, tearing up the petticoat with malice and joy, and not since she'd stolen the VanCortland name by lying and saying she was pregnant so Cort would marry her, nor since he'd divorced her and allowed her to go out on her own to annoy the world.

"Madeira Cutler," she said. "I want my glass shoe inkwell back."

"It's not yours. Cort got it in your divorce settlement. He gave it to his new daughter-in-law—my sister Sherry—who gave it to me for being her maid of honor, because I'd always loved it." I knew that the inkwell would match the one described on the scavenger hunt list—that the family it was stolen from might identify it—and prove Deborah's duplicity to a larcenous T. At the very *least*, she and her scavenging friends had obstructed justice, though to be honest, I didn't know the statute of limitations on such crimes. And however much I loved the memento of Sherry's wedding, I'd soon be turning it over to the police. "We have bigger fish to fry," I said.

"Like who?" she asked.

"Well," I said, "you."

"Me?" she squeaked.

"Sure, we have to make sure your dress fits for the *This Is Your Life* segment of the ball, now don't we?"

Werner nodded. "Mad can't wait to see what her parents uncover about your past."

Deborah paled. "Maybe I should withdraw," she said to herself.

"And never have your friends aware that you were chosen?" I knew which buttons to push.

She primped. "Hurry up and fit me. I have a hair appointment in twenty minutes. Gotta look smashing for the ball."

I smirked. Smashing and fit and ready to be handcuffed.

Twenty-nine

The creative part of fashion has always worked alongside the creative forces that have defined and colored a decade, an era. As much as art, fashion is a manifestation of the times—of its psychological, social, political, visual existence.

—IRENE SHARAFF (AMERICAN COSTUME
DESIGNER FOR STAGE AND SCREEN)

Deborah came out of the dressing room wearing the peach gown with chevron stripes and stepped onto my round dais.

I proceeded to fit her to her gown.

Chakra toyed with the petticoats and made Deborah so fidgety that I had to go in *deep* and get my happy cat out from where she was rolling on Deborah's feet while toying with the tulle beneath the dress.

Werner, from his seat in the dressing room—the husband/significant other seat—kissed his fingers when I backed out on all fours. He'd had a connoisseur's view of my nether end.

I chuckled, but Deborah huffed, because Werner's attention had not been on her, and I got back to work. "I have to let it out a bit," I said. "But not much, after forty years. Congrats."

"That and the Spanx should do it," she added.

"Maybe a protein drink for breakfast and lunch until the event?" I suggested.

She harrumphed.

Werner kept his detective's face on, but I could read the amused twinkle in his eyes.

I looked at him as I began to twirl away, and put my fingers to my lips in a farewell kiss.

Before long, I saw a dance floor from a balcony above it. The person I watched, from my vantage point *inside* Deborah VanCortland, was the late Robin O'Dowd. Deborah hated her with a passion.

One could suffocate surrounded by so much hate.

Well, Robin was more beautiful than Deborah, and though she had a man's adoration, other men also flocked around her.

Wynona ambled over to us. "Give it up, Deborah. He's hers."

"He should be mine." *Deborah had been trying to take other women's men since I'd met her. I guess it held true. Rich brat, rich bitch.*

"You wouldn't *have* him anyway. He'd be overseas all the time."

Deborah huffed. "How can I break them up? Tonight. *Keep* them apart? Just for kicks."

I felt sick in such a dark soul.

A man old enough to be Deborah's father walked by.

Deborah grabbed his hand, but he didn't turn to her, as if he shouldn't be seen with her, like maybe they were . . . having an affair? "Hey, big guy," she said. "See item seventeen on the scavenger list? Try earning those points with flyboy's girl, will you, so *I* can have some time with *him*?"

I couldn't see the guy's face, only part of a hand with the beginning of a scar that might just continue down between thumb and index finger. "My kind of sport," he said, and if the scar did extend as far as I suspected, I could identify the speaker.

They were altering people's lives, he and Vainglory, about to kill, a deadly accident likely caused by their utter selfishness. I wished Deborah could be arrested for the premeditated act of "grand theft lover."

The man in the very expensive tux went down and spirited Robin away from the dance floor. I saw him get them drinks at the patio bar. Wynona kept flyboy busy flirting. *She* kept him from looking for his girl.

The airman finally abandoned his drink, and as Deborah leaned forward to call his name, she slipped and we fell a little too far over the balcony rail, teetering just enough to make people scream . . . and allow her accomplice to spirit Robin out of the room.

The scream became a siren in my head—Deborah's head, with me inside her. When we caught our balance, and opened our eyes, the dance floor had shifted and changed, for me at least.

I stared down into the belly of the whale, which I now knew was that dirty old brick mill, in better shape back then. A sunrise lit the scene. The morning after. Everyone bedraggled. Tuxman was indeed Wayne. I'd seen *him* more clearly in the other morning-after vision, a few hours later than this, possibly, though in this same mill, the word "steam" on the inside brick wall being my touchstone.

Not that I recognized any other faces—forty years had changed them, body shapes, hairlines, and all.

Except for Grody, better known as Eric McDowell, who looked like he'd slept, or swam, in his tux. No wonder I'd named him Grody.

The stench of the sea remained as the night before, but the stench of guilt was ebbing. Daylight brought rationalizations and acceptance. "I won't tell, if you don't." And "What if she had been walking along the shore when a huge wave . . ."

The view of them was, however, so sharp that one aspect struck me like a bolt of lightning: their shoes. Most wore formal footwear, heels and stockings, except for one tuxedoed chap who wore neither socks nor wingtips, but a well-worn, wet pair of sturdy Sebago boat shoes.

Behold the sailor. Behold the blood that had dried dripping down his hand and the hand of one other in the group.

I couldn't get a name before I got whisked back to the present, to my shop's dressing room, where Deborah continued to talk about herself and her accomplishments as if nothing had happened to any of us.

Werner, though, sat straight up in the lounge chair on full alert, watching me like he wanted to scoop me into his arms, right there in the chair.

I sent him a virtual kiss, with a here-I-am nod.

He saw I'd returned, fell against the back of his chair, and wiped his brow with a trembling hand.

"Take off your jacket, Detective, if you're too warm."

"Don't mind if I do."

"You're all set, Deborah. You can go change," I said. "Detective, come with me." I reached behind me for his hand, and he clutched mine. Then, around the corner from the dressing rooms, I backed him against the wall to the enclosed stairs and kissed him senseless, or he kissed me, or we kissed each other, each with something different to prove.

He wrapped his arms around me and held me against his shoulder while he kissed my ear, then he placed his brow to mine, his breathing thready. "I have never been so scared in my life."

"I learned a few things," I said.

"That you're my Achilles' heel?"

"That, too." I couldn't help the grin that split my face. Being so cherished was new to me. Not by family, but by a significant other who didn't jaunt off and not call for months. "I learned that and more."

He set me back half a step so he could look into my eyes. "Like what?"

"How they'd spirited Robin away."

"Is that you being psychic?" Werner asked.

"No, just the psychometric facts, sir."

He closed his eyes and shook his head. "I gotta get back to the station."

I cupped his cheek. "My instincts say to find out who was still in the belly of the whale the next morning and why. Leave me the pictures and rosters so I can match names with faces, then I'll call you."

"I'll leave the pictures, but bad news, Mad. There's not one of Robin."

"They stole the evidence?" I said.

"Fifty years is a long time," Werner said. "Thatcher could have done it when he became chairman."

I bit my lip for a disappointed minute. "Wait. She was

214

presumed dead, so I presume the police looked for her before that happened, right? So maybe you have the pictures of her in your old records department."

"The basement. But I looked. Nothing on Robin O'Dowd."

The two people coming out of the shower, me covered by an airman's jacket. "Look for records on Robin Gilchrist."

"What do you know?"

"Vision—not worthy of evidence. At some point, Robin married her airman in secret, I believe, and the police who investigated after the . . . quote 'rogue wave' . . . might have figured that out."

"Mad, are you here?" Aunt Fiona called from the door.

"Coming, Aunt Fee."

Werner kissed me quick and let me go.

Deborah caught us at it. Her look said there was no accounting for taste, as she left with a silent afterthought of a wave.

"Right back at'cha," I said.

Aunt Fiona carried a garment bag and looked guilty for it. "I know you're busy, dear, and I'm here to help as much as I can, but I need a favor. I want to wear this to the Valentine's ball, and it's a little big."

"Let's see."

She took it from the garment bag and hung it on an empty rack.

"Oh, Fee, it's gorgeous, but is it—?"

"My mother's wedding dress. I always wanted to wear it for my own wedding, but let's face it: Your dad is never going to propose. He likes things the way they are."

"Surprise him. Have a party, invite a justice of the peace, wear that. He'll beg you to make it permanent."

"I don't want to coerce him into marriage, dear. I want him to want me, till death do us part."

"Is he stubborn or what, my dad?"

"Oh, speaking about weddings, and the nonstarters like mine, I wanted to share something we uncovered in our *This Is Your Life* research."

"Tell, tell."

"Eric McDowell used to be engaged to Robin O'Dowd."

"Hell-o."

"Good sleuthing, Fiona," Werner said. "Mad, I have to go back to work." His hand caressed the nape of my neck and my eyes closed at the loveliness of his touch.

Fee cleared her throat. Werner cleared his throat, too, in embarrassment, I thought, as I walked him to the door.

"Lytton, can you look up a fifty-year line of ownership to the boat named the *Yacht Sea*? The pleasure craft, not the fishing boat." I felt the heat on my face for my stupid mistake.

"Will do," he said.

"I had really hoped you'd bring me a picture of Robin. I only got a quick glimpse when I zoned."

Aunt Fee gasped. "Mad? He knows?"

Werner rolled his eyes. "Why does everybody say that?"

Aunt Fee touched his sleeve. "Because it means that your relationship must be serious. And not everybody loves her enough to believe her."

"Serious, yes, and of course I love her enough to believe her." Werner eyed me like I might be a giant Fudgsicle. Oh, I could feel the licks. Wicked thought.

"I at least hope I can find a match to Jay's father's photo in the batch you brought. Here's a copy for you. I have my own." I slipped it from my seventies-orange swing dress pocket and handed it to him.

"Wanna go dancing tonight?" he asked. "There's a rock and roll club not far from the casino."

"Can we request 'Running Bear'?" I grinned. "Around seven?"

He hooked my hair behind my ear, kissed my lobe, and whispered, "Bring an overnight bag." Then he left.

Before I started on Fee's mother's wedding gown, I moved Jay's uniform to the to-be-altered rack. As I did, the hem of the jacket swung oddly my way and hit my hip, rather too hard to be made of fabric.

I hung it then searched the pockets. A breast pocket was entirely unsewn. I slipped my hand down through the open bottom and searched around in the hem. That's when I found it. Metal and fabric. I pulled it out.

"Aunt Fee, look at this. Some kind of medal."

"Some kind . . . it's a Purple Heart, dear."

"Does that mean Jay's father's dead?"

"I don't know, dear. You tell me."

"I can't read objects."

"I thought maybe the ribbon."

I shrugged. "Not getting anything. Let me put it in my purse so you can show me that gown."

Fee's mother's wedding gown was a fifties beauty, with three-quarter sleeves, a wide fifties lace-shawl collar, cinched waist, and large lace flowers around the flared, ankle-length hem with leaf fronds that flowed three-quarters of the way up the skirt. Pure white with layers of white tulle poufed beneath. A breathtaking fashion statement for a beautiful and loving bride. *Tulle death do us part.*

"I assume that the veil became the train?" I asked.

"Yes, it's got a pristine pillbox hat that's packed away in my back closet. I don't want to give your dad a heart attack. He probably won't even realize this is a wedding gown. It's nothing like today's gowns or even the satin beauty your mother wore. Hers always reminded me of the gown that Julie Andrews wore in *The Sound of Music*."

"You're different people. If I were to pick a vintage gown, though, I'd pick this one—no offense, Mom," I said, looking up and around until I smelled the sudden scent of chocolate. Fee's eyes glistened.

"Fee. she's happy for you."

"Well, your dad hasn't asked to marry me, so *she* has nothing to worry about."

"Mom, give him a kick where it counts, will you?" I called. "Get him moving on this."

We laughed until we both had to dab our eyes.

Eve came back to help. She sorted dozens of outfits and thanked me numerous times for her Valentine date. Eventually, I chose the final three outfits for the *This Is Your Life* segment of the Very Vintage Valentine ball. They were all formals that were, to my knowledge, not connected to the scavenger hunt, aka the Robin O'Dowd case.

Frankly, things were beginning to percolate in my mind, and I wanted to run a few errands. I did some mighty thinking while driving. "Aunt Fee, can you call the next three *This Is Your Life*rs and tell them to come for fittings tomorrow? Schedule them for the morning, if possible. I need all the time I can get. The event is creeping up on us fast, and it would be helpful to have tomorrow afternoon to work on the alterations."

I drove to Aunt Fee's house in search of my father and found him in the backyard singing Italian opera at the top of his lungs while building the herbal potting shed of her dreams.

I crossed my arms and watched, standing stock still to absorb the wonder of this man, who practically raised his four chilren alone. How lucky was I?

He spotted me and clamped his lips tight, looking like a shy pup. "Hey, Madeira. Didn't see you."

"No kidding. But why be shy about it? You sing in the shower, you know."

He shook his head and swooped in for a hug. "What brings you home in the middle of the day?"

"Well, this may be your home, but mine is down the street until Alex and Trish move in."

"I mean, the neighborhood type of home."

"No, you didn't. You think of this as home now, and that's okay. Dad, we have got to talk."

"You want to move in with your detective?"

"When the time's right, and speaking of timing . . ."

"Uh-oh."

"You listen, I'll talk. No quotes allowed."

We went inside and sat on the sofa together. I took his hand. He squeezed it occasionally and took my observations well, I must say, even if they came with a rap on the knuckles, though I added a kiss to soften my blow.

He looked rattled when he stood, but he went to his jacket pocket and took something out.

"Fee should see these first, but I couldn't stand you thinking that I would do what you told me to."

I chuckled because I'm the same way.

He opened a paper and handed it to me.

"A marriage license? Fee signed it but she doesn't know what it is, does she?"

"No, and don't you tell her. I tricked her. I told her it was the building permit for the potting shed to get her to sign."

I screamed at the top of my lungs and threw myself at him. He twirled me, and I adored the robust sound of his laughter. *Oh, Mom, he's happy again.*

"How you gonna do it?" I asked.

"I don't know."

"Can I see inside that tiny square box?"

"No. This, Fee gets to see first, and she never *ever* hears about this talk, got it?"

I raised a hand. "You beat me to the punch."

"Damn straight I did."

He set an arm around my shoulders. " 'While we try to teach our children all about life, our children teach us what life is all about.' Angela Schwindt said that. Thanks for caring enough to try, kiddo."

After I left my father, I went back to the house to get ready for my date and overnight with Werner.

First thing the next morning, after a Werner-specialty homemade breakfast, I set Fee and Dolly up at the shop, and went to look at the *Yacht Sea* in its slip at the marina, hoping for clues to a forty-year-old personal attack. Instead

I found Eric McDowell himself—in grungy jeans on his knees shining brass.

"You're into boats these days, Ms. Cutler?"

"You heard that I got covered in fish on the *Yacht C*?"

"Yes," he said on a chuckle. "I presume you were sleuthing and thought you'd found this boat, since the old scavenger hunt case is open again. You know, fishermen rarely join the country club. You didn't notice that there was a *Yacht A* and a *Yacht B* beside it?"

I took a deep breath, calling myself: stupid, stupid, stupid. "It was dark."

"So I hear. At any rate, I would have given you the tour of this McDowell yacht at anytime." He offered me his arm so I could climb aboard.

"I realize that now. You know, Councilman, you have always confused me."

"You feel like dusting for prints, don't you? Go ahead. Need help? I'm your man."

He indicated that I should precede him as if I could wander around the luxury yacht at will.

"I was a suspect once, wasn't I?" he asked. "Maybe I am again?"

"Maybe you took part in that old scavenger hunt."

His brows furrowed and he crossed his arms to lean against the rail. "I don't know how, but you *know* that I did, which is not an admission of guilt where Ms. O'Dowd was concerned."

"Maybe. I like this boat. It has a history," I said to gauge his reaction. "Zavier loves it. You must be glad your father got him out on bail this morning. Where are you going?" I asked as McDowell swung himself over the rail and off his boat in one leap.

"To protect my brother, I'll get custody if I have to."

McDowell wanted to take Zavier away from their father? Why? I called Werner to share that bit of news and barely finished when I got another caller beeping in. I said a quick "bye, love you" to Werner and took the next call.

"Mad," Eve said. "I had dinner at Jay's last night. His grandmother is kind of psychic like him, and she knows a lot about the fiftieth. You might want to trump up a reason to go there and talk to her."

"You never send me out sleuthing, Eve. What's with you today?"

"Whatever you uncover might help Jay find his dad. I'd like to see that happen for him, 'kay?"

"You're smitten."

"From the minute I laid eyes on him. You knew that."

"I did but I wanted to hear you admit it."

I didn't need to trump up anything more than a Purple Heart, thanks to a cooperative universe. Jay's father had been wounded. He might even be dead.

I set my Garmin for Jay's address. This global positioning system was the answer to my prayers. Every directionally-challenged person should own one. With it, I took a ride to Rhode Island to meet the grandmother who raised Jay, Airman Gilchrist, so well.

When his grandmother came to the door, my last hope for finding a living Robin O'Dowd vanished. Fee and my dad were in their early sixties. Jay's grandmother might be Ethel Sweet's peer, early eighties.

"Mrs. Gilchrist, my name is Madeira Cutler. I'm from Mystic."

"Vintage Magic, right? You fit my grandson to his father's uniform yesterday morning. You made a positive and lasting impression on him."

"The feeling was mutual. As a matter of fact, he's taking my best friend to the country club event. We're double dating."

"Eve, yes. I met her last night. You're not as darkly dressed as she is."

How kind she was. I chuckled as Mrs. Gilchrist led me into a house straight out of the seventies. Red maple furniture, ruffled lampshades, a spinning wheel in the corner. In the open kitchen, harvest gold appliances and knotty pine cabinets. "Chai tea?" she asked, a trend almost too much with the times in this place. "Can I interest you in a fresh lemon square? Still warm."

I was suddenly ten and she was Dolly Sweet trying to make me forget that I'd lost my mother.

"This is a home, not a house," I said. "You're making me feel like company instead of a stranger."

"Do you have a problem with that?"

"Yes, guilt. I wanted to ask you about the Mystick Country Club's fiftieth. Eve said you might be able to help with the investigation, though I do have something for you." I set the Purple Heart on the cobbler's bench coffee table between us. "I found it in the lining of your son's airman's uniform."

She picked it up lovingly, although her expression was shocked. "I didn't know. He was awarded a Purple Heart and then went missing soon after. I had no idea that Glen survived, and came back home, only to disappear again." She took out a linen handkerchief with a crochet edging and wiped her eyes.

I let my throat work to keep me from joining her.

The woman with her hair in a gray bun and Victorian combs holding it together stood resolutely, went into the kitchen, and silently made me a chai tea, though I hadn't said yes. And now she set a plate of lemon squares between us and sat in a big overstuffed chair across from me. I could tell she was still processing the news, but she seemed determined to remain in an upbeat mood. "Jay is an excellent judge of character, and your friend Eve is the first girl he's ever taken home for dinner then talked about for so long after bringing her home."

"We might have a match, but . . . well, she marches to her own drummer."

"More than me with my old-fashioned taste? I'm disappointed."

"A lot more."

"Locks on her ankle straps, black and copper, goth, right?"

We laughed. "Really, why sit still for my questions, Mrs. Gilchrist? Especially after the news I shared with you."

"One, I'm polite. Two, they reopened the scavenger-hunt case and the detective is your boyfriend, yes?"

"Yes."

She raised her chin. "Well, as my grandson is fond of saying, granite is granite, impervious, no matter how hard you try to break it, unless you have the right tools to cut into it, make something beautiful of it."

"I don't understand."

She pulled back the curtain and I saw the stonecutter next door, headstones lined the yard. I had parked on the other side, so this was my first sight of it.

"Family business. My oldest nephew runs it for me," she said. "We use granite a lot in metaphors around here."

Thirty

As I drove home from Scituate, I realized that my trip had netted me some extra background information for our *This Is Your Life* segment.

Instead of going home I went directly to the police station.

"Billings," I said, going in. "Is your boss—"

"Go right in, Mad," Billings said.

"Don't you have to announce me so he can complain—"

"New rule. You get to go right in, if he's not interrogating a perp or answering to a government official. As for complaining, he hasn't chewed any of us out in a couple'a weeks, thanks to you."

I sailed right by him and into Werner's office. He didn't even look up, so I shut his door, easy-like.

He looked up but his frown turned to a grin.

226

I grinned as well, in anticipation, as he came toward me. I had never been pinned against this particular door before.

When we came up for air, I remembered him shutting the file in front of him when he saw me.

He now shook his head. "The O'Dowd case really doesn't add up. I wish I knew who the guy you call Snake was."

"That's looking possible all of a sudden."

"How can we make it a viable fact?"

"As in motivation, means, opportunity? Get this . . ."

I told Werner the details of how another puzzle accidently fell into place that could help lead us to that viable fact and I got another kiss for my brilliance.

"See?" I said. "Me sleuthing has perks."

"Try reminding me about that the *next* time I pull you from the bottom of a well."

"That's old news," I said. "Have I been as sloppy in recent years or during recent cases?"

"I plead the fifth," he said

I threw my arms around him and we held to the embrace, our cheeks pressed together. Just content to hold on. Something else new to my life.

I hated to break the moment, but we had a case to solve and I had an idea that came with a timeline and a ticking clock. "You had an appointment with Eric McDowell today, didn't you?" I asked, as a reason to step back and toy with my guy's tie. "Did you find out why he wants custody of his brother, Zavier? Gimme details."

"Details I got, but they have no basis in fact."

Proving things was our—Werner's—job. "Suppose you

interview all the suspects one more time and ask one more question."

"Ah," he said, nodding, his mind working.

"After you do that," I said, "you'll either have straight answers or reactions, all of which will be reason enough to bring it to the final segment of *This Is Your Life*."

"In front of all those people?"

"I was thinking that we should move the dancing to before dinner, even through cocktails, so people can get the celebrating out of their systems. We have five guests that are, let's face it—after perusing Dad and Fee's backgrounds on them and their surprise guests—rather anticlimactic. By then, the attendees might want to go home."

Werner grabbed his all-weather coat and opened his door so I could precede him out.

"What are you doing?"

"We're going home."

"Why?"

Werner roared. "You still have to ask?"

Werner started my car, and left his in the lot. "I think that our attendees won't want to be rude, even if we do want them to go."

"Call an intermission and give them an escape route. You know that half of them will go."

"Half of them is good."

"It really turns me on that you understand my job," he said, pulling into his driveway.

We ate a late dinner, then we went for a moonlight stroll and got back to our earlier conversation.

"I must admit that your plan is almost perfect," Werner said.

"We have no choice," I replied, "except to surprise our last entrant with an unexpected reading and as unexpected a past as possible, or it won't work, except that really, *This Is Your Life* isn't our party to alter."

Werner stopped and turned to me. "You think your father and Fee would let us run the show instead of them?"

I hit speed dial on my phone, asked Fiona, who relayed the question to my dad, got my answer, and slipped my cell back into my pocket. "To quote my dad: 'In a New York minute.'"

"Tomorrow and this weekend I have to return the unchosen formals while you interview our scavenger-hunt lot. Wish I could be with you."

"I can't believe that Sunday, we're on." He pulled me against his side. "We make a good team, kid."

I usually shied away from any "team" statement that came from a member of the opposite sex, but this time, getting closer seemed the thing to do.

"Our version of *This Is Your Life* is starting to look like a sting operation," I said.

"I'll put officers in formal dress and pepper the audience with them."

"It'll be more entertaining than . . . well . . . a scavenger hunt. It also makes me think of the game Mousetrap— Snap. Snap. Snap.

"I can hardly wait."

"Only one loose cannon to worry about," Werner said.

"Who?"

"Wynona has a ticket to the ball, and frankly she's got a couple billion motives for wanting Wayne dead. I'm looking forward to talking with her tomorrow."

"Dollars?" I confirmed.

He shrugged and I understood. Cutting too close to the need-to-know bone for a detective.

"If she is her husband's killer, be careful, she's dangerous." I took another step, then turned back to him. "She would have had the same motive for wanting Robin dead, wouldn't she . . . if she were planning to reel Wayne in."

"Yep, it always comes down to money."

"Where have I heard that before?"

The next morning, after Eve left with the first batch of unchosen formal returns, I called Werner. "I have a confession to make," I said. "I forgot to tell you last night with everything else, but I still have scavenged items at my Dad's. Forgot about them between Wayne's death, the new us, fitting formals, and our plan to net a whale this weekend."

Werner cleared his throat. "Madeira? Where did you get the newest scavenged items?"

"Some were in that drainpipe you uncapped. Jammed into the end you were holding. Found them by accident. The others I found at the warehouse before the fishing boat incident. We went there specifically to retrieve them. I'd seen them get hidden in a vision."

"If you're going to keep sleuthing, Mad—"

"Last night, you said I was good at it. Talking with a different brain today, are you?"

He chuckled.

"I am a sleuth. There'll be no talking me out of it."

"Then let me in on the visions. Beforehand, maybe?"

"As your significant other, I understand the request. But sometimes I have to base my decisions on the fact that you're a detective and may not want me to go where I need to. And sometimes, as you saw, they just happen."

Werner growled low in his throat, like when he wanted to ravish me.

"When I plan a vision, I'll try to inform you, so you can be with me, 'kay?"

"Let's sort that out later. I maybe went too far," he admitted. "I can see there'd be exceptions, but for my invested part, your safety as well as justice have to be served."

"Justice is always my primary goal."

"Your safety is mine," he grumbled. "You're starting to feel like a full-time job."

"That's bad?"

"No, it's good. When I'm here, I want to be there."

"And vice versa," I admitted. "Except that we live in the real world."

"Shame, that. But on the other hand, I might want to leave the force to be with you."

I chuckled at the tongue-in-cheek comment. "We'd kill each other if we spent too much time together. You love the force, plus we can partner-sleuth best with you on the inside."

"It's a tricky business, though, unless—"

"What?" I asked.

"Mystick Falls is about to need a new mayor," he said.

"I was thinking of running, but you should run, and I'll stay on as detective."

I chuckled. "Which would make me your immediate boss."

"Go ahead, Mad, tell me what to do. Like you don't already try."

"Like there aren't times you like it. But be serious."

"Oh, I am. Sleuthing would take on the sheen of your position, the mayor getting nosy for the greater good. I could be your trusty knight in shining armor."

I shivered. "This is starting to sound kinky."

"Yeah, I like that aspect of it, too. Think about it."

"Could I be mayor and keep the shop?" *Like I'd actually consider it . . .*

"Sure, but I'd suggest a full-time assistant."

"The universe is speaking to me again," I said. "Isobel York, my former intern, sent me a job application last week."

"She was excellent, too, wasn't she?" Werner asked. "It's a sign. With her working for you, we might actually be able to get away for the occasional weekend."

"Are we moving too fast?" I asked.

"Are you getting cold feet, Mad? I'll warm them. Or I'll back off. Your call. I've been waiting since you came home to set up your shop. I've been dreaming of you since we shared a bed that lovely night at Kyle DeLong's in New York."

"You think getting Tasered is lovely?"

"The result being our first—indelibly stamped on *my* libido—thermonuclear kiss. *Shockingly* lovely. I've heard that you bragged about it on occasion, even when we weren't a couple."

I'd wring Eve's neck later. "*I* haven't been able to forget our rock and roll fling," I admitted. "I guess I've been really dense, haven't I?"

"It didn't help that your sister Sherry played matchmaker by making you and Nick her twins' godparents. Even I saw through that."

"So you stepped back . . . to wait for me to figure it out?"

"We wouldn't have made a very good couple if I was the only one who knew that. Sure, I bided my time. You're a girl who appreciates home. I knew you'd find home in my arms."

"And in your bed?"

"You can't be seducing me over the phone, Mad. You're killing me, here."

"It's awfully easy."

He growled in that "gotta have you now" way of his, the one that shivered me to my core. "Gotta get back to work," he said. "Wear something fifties for dancing."

"What color underwear?"

"Make it match, of course." And he hung up.

I smiled through the dozen formals that ended up back at my shop with their owners that afternoon to be fitted for the event. Once they knew they hadn't been chosen, many of the entrants decided to attend our Very Vintage Valentine ball anyway, and wear the outfit they'd entered in the competition.

All the while I worked, I thought about Werner and his final interviews with the suspects.

The returning windfall of tulle turned Chakra into a ballet cat, tiptoeing through the tullelips and sniffing every one, not forgetting the occasional purring roll or kitty joust.

Through the afternoon, several *This Is Your Life* rejects, not going to the ball after all, offered me the formals they didn't want anymore. I bought eight, and put aside one in mocha for me, and one in black-and-white for Eve, because they fit our personalities so much better than our original choices.

Not quite steampunk goth, Eve's was a full-length vintage seventies gown in black-and-ivory organdy. But the fitted bodice with velvet trim and a single halter strap that crossed at the top's point and made its way around her neck in one piece represented Eve the seductress quite well. Its full flared skirt with diamond-shaped panels graduating from black at the waist to ivory at the hem came with two tulle crinolines. What I liked best for Eve was the boned bodice that gave her dress a shape reminiscent of a bustier, boned at the sides and wired at the top.

I adored the gown I picked for myself, an Emma Domb mocha tulle and lace that gave my curls the sheen of cinnamon at my shoulders. The strapless, heart-shaped, lace bodice had a ruffled inset of fine mocha net and coarse tulle. I felt like a confection when I tried it on. The lace formed a double layer overtop that accented my breasts, trimmed in chocolate sequins, also like a bustier, to a deep, almost Elizabethan V ending well below the waist. Then it defied convention and flowed like a double overskirt in an inverted V away from the waist. The topmost overskirt ended about six inches higher than the one below it, eighteen inches from the hem. My bodice was also boned. I'd think rose gold and copper jewelry, though if I wasn't careful, I'd hit the steampunk mark, which I wouldn't do to my BFF on purpose.

Suddenly I couldn't wait for Werner to see me in it.

After Dad had told me his secret, he'd called later that night to tell me he'd like to add one last portion to our evening. He wanted to give a party after the ball at my shop for a small number of family and friends, but he didn't want Fiona to know. He even asked what caterer I'd trust setting up while we were at the ball, and we got that settled.

Since I knew he had an engagement ring that Fiona was not yet wearing, I hoped he planned to propose and throw Fee an engagement party. But, nah, Dad would never do anything so prosaic. Never something so intimate in public.

Not in a million years.

Otherwise, I knew the stage was set.

I was so excited that the clocked ticked slower. Friday, Saturday, and Sunday morning, I filled with altering and being there so people could collect their formals.

When Sunday, the night of the ball, finally arrived, Dad and Fee looked great as a couple. Dad in his gray tux with tails, no less, and a lavender tie. Fiona, in her mother's wedding gown, though she'd worn it with lavender shoes, a lavender pillbox hat, and a lavender velvet bow around her waist.

Though we were nervous, we joined the dancing for a requested round of "Running Bear," and a lot of people rocked and rolled. The night was turning out to be everything I had imagined.

After dinner, I gave out small prizes to the people who'd worn the best vintage outfits, just as Aunt Fee had originally planned. Once dessert came, Werner and I got up on stage to began the *This Is Your Life* segment of the program. We revealed the lives of the innocents first, sort of as practice, and that part of the program held just the right amount of surprises and reasons to applaud. There were even a couple of standing ovations and plenty of hankies being used to dab at wet eyes. Big success. So far.

"Deborah is a no-show," I told Werner.

"Not surprised," Werner said. "She did not like my line of questioning on Friday. I think she's afraid of what we've learned during the investigation."

"What if you need her to testify?"

"We'll find her," my hunky detective promised with an impromptu kiss to my brow that melted me just a bit.

Eve and Jay had come to dinner at Werner's Friday night—a fun double date—and after having received the gift of his dad's Purple Heart from his grandmother, Jay had happily given up his *This Is Your Life* spot for our surprise guest.

The ballroom had been decorated to an understated elegance. Large gold rings hooked together in strategic places, especially around the architectural model for the new wing of the country club. They'd be lucky if it didn't close down after what we were about to reveal.

Werner called for an intermission and a last bar call before the final segment. Everybody groaned, but the bar was soon packed. I knew that plainclothes policemen ringed the room, fake drinks in hand so as not to look conspicuous. Werner and I quickly had a last meeting with our surprise guests—the "Remember Me?" type—and made sure the unsuspecting subject of our last *This Is Your Life* segment still sat at his reserved table. He was too important to walk out.

As my father had requested, I asked Aunt Fiona to help backstage while he slipped out the door early. He took Dolly Sweet, wearing her Katharine Hepburn gown, with him. Yes, the gown she planned to die in. Always a heart-attack event for me when she wore it, but as her laughter followed her out the door, I sighed with relief. She'd made it through another big event unscathed. Whew. At 106, one never knew.

Eve and Jay, looking dapper in his dad's uniform, left our deserted table, and switched to a table where another man in an airman's dress uniform sat alone.

The first thing the stranger did was check out Jay's Purple Heart, and as I passed the table, Jay explained that it wasn't his; it was his dad's, which got them to chatting.

At the break, there'd been a bit of a mass exodus and the place was still slowly emptying to a very comfortable degree. The plainclothes policemen knew who to encourage to go and those who needed to stay. Sometimes I saw a badge being discreetly revealed. We did not want to play the sting to an audience of hundreds, just to a few friends who might later testify.

With a Shirley Temple in hand, I went back over to say hello to Eve and Jay and thank both him and their new table partner for serving our country.

Frankly, we were trying to stall. We had wanted Wynona

to be one of our guests, but she was unable to make it. I guessed that Werner injected fear into our suspects at his Friday interrogation. She'd just been arrested in Montauk and they were now sending her back on the New London Ferry. Werner sent a Mystick Falls black-and-white to pick her up and bring her here.

"They've got Wynona," he updated me as I returned backstage.

"What will happen to her?"

"She's been arrested for the murder of her husband," he said, "though I don't know if I can make it stick, but she's been told we'll go easier on her if she helps us get to the truth here. She took the bait. They're bringing her here. I mean, she implicated herself by running, so she gave us a stronger case against her."

"Let's hope she cooperates when it comes right down to it," I said. "But why did she flee Mystick Falls today and not right after the interrogation?" I asked.

Werner gave me a double take. "One, she knew we'd be busy tonight, and it would be easier for her to run. And two, a wife disappearing immediately after her husband's murder is just too suspicious. She tried to play it cool."

"Now that she'll be here after all, do we need her to get started?"

"No, we'll use her when they get her here."

I rubbed my hands together. "Good. Let's go."

I had no sooner said it and the lights dimmed as everyone began to return to their seats. Meanwhile, our mark continued celebrating and having a fine time.

"Ladies and gentlemen," Werner said, "our final contestant suggested we honor someone who has been a touchstone for all of us here at the Mystick by the Sea Country Club, Mr. Thatcher McDowell. Let's stand and put our hands together so he'll know how *much* we want him up here."

And, holy slip stitch, did we want Thatcher in the hot seat.

Thatcher beamed as a waiter brought his favorite, most expensive choice of beverage up on stage with a fine Cuban cigar to set on the table beside the big, overstuffed burgundy leather easy chair, with a matching ottoman, that we'd placed on stage for the segment.

"There you go," Werner said. "Put your feet up, make yourself comfortable."

Let us help you forget what a beast you are, I thought. *For the moment.*

The music died down, and we got to work. I opened the large *Life* book, which looked just like the one every host of the original *This Is Your Life* show had used. "Tell us, Thatcher, if you remember this voice," I said.

A spotlight hit the blank stage curtain.

"You hired me for the twenty-fifth jubilee and fired me on the fiftieth."

Thatcher chuckled. "How unkind of me. No, I don't know the voice."

We led our surprise guest out. A waiter.

"Why did I fire you?" Thatcher asked.

"Because you were undressing a member of the waitstaff in your office, sir, and I walked in on you."

Thatcher winked. "It was *her* idea, but we'll be gentlemen about it, shall we? Tell you what, you can have your old job back. Double pay."

"I'm ninety-seven years old, sir." The old man bowed. "I'll start tomorrow."

The son of a gun got a big laugh as he left the stage and the audience applauded with enthusiasm.

"How about this voice?" Werner asked Thatcher.

"I helped you twice at the fiftieth jubilee, once here in the ballroom, and once to lure Robin onto your boat, the *Yacht Sea*."

That voice surprised me because I hadn't realized Wynona had arrived. Werner winked at me. Thatcher seemed even more surprised than I was.

"Wynona, what the dickens are you talking about?" Thatcher insisted, uncomfortably.

She stepped onto the stage rubbing her wrists, with two officers at attention on either side of her, about three feet back. "I'm talking about the scavenger hunt, and what you wanted most."

Thatcher's laugh became a little less robust.

"I don't know what you're talking about."

"We assured Robin that the whole gang was playing a practical joke on the party back at the country club, and we were meeting on your boat. We told her it had to do with the scavenger hunt. But you zipped away from the dock the minute we stepped onboard, then you gave the wheel to Eric and went at her."

Werner gave a motion that implied *back-up-but-stay-alert* to the officers. They complied, as did Wynona.

I turned the page on the book of *Life*, and half expected it to begin to smolder. "Hear this voice, Thatcher McDowell."

From behind the curtain we heard: "You made me take the blame." The man's voice spoke with a bit of a whine. "You even made me hide the cash box in the attic of the Underhill building all those years ago, and I was scared, but I kept my toys, even if you said to throw 'em away, they'll get you in trouble if anyone finds them."

"Well, now see," Thatcher said, "that's my Zavier. You know how he is. You can't go listening to anything he says."

Zavier came out with his here-I-am smile, and because he seemed to expect it, people applauded, giving him a bit of the limelight. He'd always been a special friend to the people of Mystic. He'd help anybody with anything. He was often included in picnics and special events just so he felt like he had a life.

What we did not expect our shy boy to do was shake his fist at his dad, then poke an accusing finger into the old man's chest. "And those sex things you made me say I did, you take that back. Tell the truth now."

Thatcher tried to stand, but the officer nearest his chair flashed his badge. "Please remain seated, sir."

Fee led Zavier off stage and to the table with Eve, Jay, and the airman.

"How about this voice?" I asked, the tremble I felt inside becoming evident in my voice.

Eric McDowell was up next. Like the rest of them, he first spoke from behind the curtain. "On the night of the country club's fiftieth anniversary, you took the *Yacht Sea* out in a storm. That's the family boat. You weren't alone. You took Wynona, Robin, and me. Who am I?"

"Well," Thatcher said, making a show of reseating himself, but removing his legs from the hassock. "You're my son Eric, but you're a little confused, boy."

Eric came out and nobody applauded. We were getting to the sticking point, and there was nothing to celebrate.

Thatcher hit Eric with his unlit cigar. "Why'd you go and say those things, boy? Didn't I teach you better?"

"No, sir, you taught me worse. First, you made me captain your boat. Then you had Wynona help you get your hands on Robin, until I realized what you were up to. Eventually, I hit you with everything I could throw at you so Robin could escape. She ran for the rail and you followed. I know that Wynona and I were there to make it look like the party you lied about, but frankly, you're one sick son of a sea cow."

"You're making this up," Thatcher said, but he didn't sound as confident as he'd tried to be earlier.

"To defend herself she broke one of your champagne bottles, then used it to cut your hand between your thumb and forefinger," Eric said. "When you let her go to stem the blood, she jumped overboard. I didn't think she'd make it in a storm, so I lowered the lifeboat and went after her. You kept calling me to come back."

Thatcher sat forward. "See, you're all mixed up, boy. Robin, she was just walking along the rocks with her friends—they'll tell you—and she got taken by a rogue wave. It's in the records. And you've got no proof. She's gone, son."

Because my throat was working and I was trying not to blubber like a baby, Werner took over. "How about this voice, Thatcher McDowell?"

"I did not get taken by a rogue wave. Your son Eric saved my life, and that of my unborn son. He got me to shore, drove me to safety so the richest man in Mystick Falls couldn't destroy me. And later, he helped me put my son through college."

Whoa. Now that was a piece of information about Eric McDowell I didn't know. He caught my eye, and I nodded, which seemed to please him. I guessed our animosity was at an end. I had misjudged the man, but, hey, as far as the universe went, there was obviously something I'd had to figure out before we could get to this place.

"I've had enough." Thatcher stood, but two uniforms came from the shadows and helped him back into the chair, then stood guard, one on each side.

The owner of the voice Thatcher refused to acknowledge came out from behind the curtain.

"Who the hell are you?" he spat, letting us see his venom.

She wore one of the tulle formals I'd recently bought, in red, like that night, and in front of Thatcher, she put on the blonde pageboy wig I'd brought her.

Thatcher nearly had a heart attack. Werner nodded for the medics.

Forty years later, I'd found her still in hiding, wearing cropped black hair, streaked blue, dressing like a man, these days sculpting granite into important statues, under the guise of the family business.

Jay thought of his mother's heart as made of granite. I

thought she was dead. We both got a surprise when the story came out. We had both been wrong.

Robin O'Dowd was ready to be set free and live again.

"See?" she said, stepping right up to Thatcher, who had a hand to his heart. "I didn't die. I simply protected my son from the man who could destroy me for knowing *what* he really was. You were too powerful to fight against back then, even with the truth. And for the record, I'd like to say that I'm pressing charges against you for attempted, aggravated sexual assault. I had the bruises to prove it, and I still have the pictures."

Thatcher turned to his son Eric. "You let me think I murdered someone."

Eric looked down at his father without emotion. "Too bad thinking yourself a murderer didn't cause a need in you to repent, to do some good, shoulder the guilt, pay your debt to society. And who knows what you would have done, if you'd found out that Robin wasn't dead after all. I know the bad things you are capable of."

The old man suddenly needed oxygen.

Zavier rushed from the table to the edge of the stage. "Don't you die yet. You tell them first. All those bad things. *You* did 'em. Not me. Tell 'em. Tell 'em now before you die."

Eric jumped from the stage, put an arm around his brother's shoulder, led him to a table, and called for a ginger ale.

Jay and the airman, who relied heavily on a cane, approached the stage, Eve not far behind.

"Robin," the airman said. "Robin, I can't believe my eyes. Is it really you?"

"Glen? Glen!" she screamed. "You *didn't* die?"

Jay lifted his mother down off the stage then his parents, both of them, were in each other's arms, holding, confirming life, their tears contagious.

Eve sort of held Jay up, he was in shock at the scene. He'd finally found his father, and he was not missing or dead, but now more alive than ever.

"I said I'd never come back to this town," Jay's father said. "Too many bad memories, once I heard about what had happened that night. I couldn't have lived here without you, and I didn't want to live in a town where I suspected people of hurting you. But I got the country club invitation and I thought, what the hell? One more look. It had been so long." He raised an arm to include Jay. "Right off, I find my son wearing my Purple Heart. Until this minute, I thought *he* was the surprise of a lifetime, but if my son was alive, then Robin had to be as well. And now there are two of you. I've gotten back everything I thought I'd lost."

Gilchrist kissed his wife and embraced his son. It was the night of their secret wedding, right after a shower, that I'd horned in on them—and got covered with his jacket—not for long, fortunately.

Eve grinned from ear to ear. And had I just glimpsed Deborah VanCortland stepping from the shadows in the back of the room?

"It's a shame that we didn't solve the mystery before Wayne was murdered," I said to Werner as he approached me.

Werner nodded. "But if I have my way, Thatcher—"

"Also known as Snake," I informed him.

"Ah." Werner covered the microphone with a hand. "If I have my way, Thatcher and Wynona will both get put away. Wynona's a pretty sure thing. As for Thatcher, his assault on Robin won't play—time's run out—but the recent sexual attacks, for which Zavier took the fall, will now be charged to Thatcher. He also has to answer for the country club's financial games, and I'll red-flag him to the IRS regarding his personal financials."

Werner leaned toward me, lowering his voice. "I'd sure like to know if Thatcher had a hand in killing Wayne."

Wynona, at the end of the stage, stamped a foot, catching our attention.

She cleared her throat. "Wayne was getting fidgety in his old age, crying literally over his dead sister."

"Wayne wanted to know *who* sent Robin into the water. And I couldn't let him know I was there, but he kept asking questions. Too many questions. So I shut him up."

Thatcher narrowed his eyes. "You wanted me to get rid of Robin, didn't you, Wynona? One way or another you were going to see that Wayne got Robin's half of his paternal grandparents' money that night. You were always the most selfish person alive."

"Nobody can prove that," she sang.

Thatcher slapped the arms of his chair. "You told me you were gonna marry Wayne after that night's work, once you were sure he'd inherit all of the money."

"Doesn't prove a thing."

"Thanks for the confessions, both of you," Werner said into the mike.

I turned off the mike and left the stage. First I checked on Bambi-Jo, who'd screamed once, fainted twice, and needed the paramedics and oxygen, evidently.

She just kept rolling her head from side to side saying, "I didn't know, I didn't know."

What could I say? I'd been there inside her head. She sincerely did not know.

And who came walking straight into the spotlight but Deborah VanCortland? "I just wanted to see it all fall apart," she said by way of explanation. "My significant other heard on the police radio that they arrested Wynona and called me to listen. I heard them get directed here, and I knew it was time."

"Because you know more than you let on?" I asked.

"Maybe," Deborah said. "I've been selfish since I learned how to get my own way. You know about my marriage, Madeira. Years earlier, at the scavenger hunt, I figured that one of the guys had taken Robin for a fling. But I actually did believe that it all went wrong when she got taken by that rogue wave, that she wouldn't have died if we hadn't played scavenger hunt. I justified my share of guilt; I'm good at that. I didn't think Thatcher was capable of sexual assault any more than I believed Eric was capable of saving a life and protecting the good deed for a lifetime. I mean, he's a politician."

I nodded, because I agreed with her on that score.

"I did believe," Deborah, aka Vainglory, said, "that they were both as selfishly greedy as I was. I am now and probably always will be . . . a teller of tales as they suit my needs," Deborah added, almost as an afterthought. "If you want to arrest me for anything, you should arrest me because I outright lied and said that I was with Robin when that wave took her. I did it to stay popular." She looked up at Robin. "I may be a bitch, but I'm glad you made it."

Robin gave Deborah a hard half nod.

Deborah had helped steal away a lifetime of happiness for Robin with her husband and son, but Robin had too much class to point that out.

"Deborah, one of you that I interviewed talked about two other scavenger hunters. One smelled of Brut after-shave. Who was he?"

Eric raised a hand. "That was me. I always wore too much Brut."

Eric McDowell, also known as Grody to me. Another identified. "Can any of you identify Tuxman?"

"One of my best friends, and the one with the most guilt for the rest of his short life."

I turned on my heel toward Werner. "Every scavenger hunter accounted for as far as I know."

Werner scanned the crowd. "Eric, anyone? Deborah? Bambi-Jo?"

They didn't even look at each other but denied, each in their own way, the existence of any other conspirators.

"Huzzah, it's done!" Jay came my way as I left Deborah with the police. Robin's son, now Eve's date, hugged and twirled me. "I found my dad because you raised your roof! I knew there was a reason you were important to finding him."

His parents smiled and kissed again.

"Oh! Speaking of dads, I've gotta run. Hey, all of you, Robin and Glen, Eve and Jay, come to a party. It's at my shop. Eve, show them the way." I grabbed Werner's hand and ran.

Thirty-one

They really shouldn't allow a veil like this. All the men should rise in a body and make it a law for any woman not to be so attractive. It's just a frill of lace, but it has been attached to the inside of a hat, just where the crown rests on the head. It really should be stopped—men have a hard enough time in this world as it is.

—"MAKERS OF MYSTERY," *VOGUE*, 1917

My second floor had been transformed into a lavender fairyland. And there beside the orchestra was a spot for the emcee, our old friend Tunney Lague. Heck, he was everybody in town's old friend.

"Ah," Tunney said. "Our Madeira's here. Time to get this party officially under way. Harry, my old friend, has a plan, and I do believe he kept it from most of us until the very last minute. Even me. He only gave me my to-do list this morning. Nobody's as organized as old Harry."

"And nobody tells so many secrets as Tunney Lague," my dad replied. My father cleared his throat. "And let's call me young Harry for tonight, okay, my friend?"

"Will do." Tunney raised his glass. "Let's have a drink to young Harry Cutler." Our emcee smacked his lips and went back to his script.

Aunt Fee's jaw sat kind of slack. I put my fingers to her chin to raise it.

"What is he up to?" she asked.

Werner stepped in and came to our side, encircling my hand with one of his. Dante appeared and stood beside Dolly. She tittered.

"Young Harry," Tunney said, "your turn to take the floor."

My father went up the steps to a dais with a curtain behind it. "Fiona, would you please join me up here to lead the evening in the right direction?"

"Has he been drinking with Tunney?" she asked near my ear before she followed him right up there.

My sisters, I was surprised to note, were *both* here, Sherry and her husband, Justin, even Brandy with her significant other, Cort—Sherry's father-in-law, also known as Deborah's ex-husband. My brother, Alex, and his wife, Trish, too. Chairs were arranged to face the curtain up front.

Dad took Fiona in his arms and kissed her senseless forever, until the wolf whistles were making me deaf, and the drummer built to a crescendo.

Then my dad stepped back and grinned. "First surprise: I can be spontaneous. Second: I can kiss in public."

Everyone laughed.

"Watch this. I can kneel in public, too." Which he did.

Fiona slapped a hand to her mouth.

He took out a small velvet box and opened it. "Fiona Sullivan, heart of my heart, will you do me the greatest honor and become my wife, till death do us part?" He furrowed his brow. "And maybe not even, which means I'll have two of you. Wow, that's a bit scary."

The Cutler kids—me included—and Aunt Fiona, too, thought that was hilarious.

She might have been laughing, but her hands shook as he slipped the diamond on her engagement finger. "Yes," she whispered.

"We can't hear you," we chorused.

"Yes!" she shouted, and Dad rose to take her in his arms again.

"An engagement party," she said. "A surprise engagement party."

"Oh no, sweet, did you think this was over? No, no no. Go into Madeira's storage closet, will you? You'll find everything you need in there."

"Ooh, not everything." I thought I'd grabbed her veil a few days ago to bring here to fix. But had my dad put that thought into my head? Or my mom?

Fiona looked forsaken. "You're sending me away?" But she said it as she admired her engagement ring.

My father blew her a kiss. "We'll call you back when we're ready."

My brother, Alex, led her to my storage area and shut them in. I opened the door a crack to hand them the veil and was told to wait right outside the door.

A minister stepped up to the top of the dais, and Tunney pulled the curtains to reveal an arch decorated with lavender roses behind it. My dad stopped at the middle step and turned to face his guests.

Tunney instructed us to take our seats, though I stayed where I was told, by the chairs lined up in front of the arch, then Tunney cued the bandleader, and they played the traditional wedding march.

The doors to the closet opened, and five-year-old Kelsey, in a full-length gown borrowed from Sherry's wedding, led the parade straight to the dais. Behind her, Sherry, in lavender on Justin's arm, pushed a lavender decorated, twin baby stroller with Riley and Kathleen inside.

My sister Brandy and Cort followed.

After them, Alex told me to go up the aisle as maid of honor.

I waited and waved to Robin, Glen, Jay, and Eve, in the back row, all grinning, and more often than not, necking.

Then my brother, Alex, escorted our former Aunt Fiona—not really our aunt—eyes bright, her bouquet a ball of lavender roses, up the aisle. Alex handed her to my dad with a kiss and my dad and his soon to be new wife went up to meet the minister.

"Harry," Fee whispered, not knowing the minister was holding a mike. "We don't have a marriage license."

"Yes we do."

"*I* never signed one."

"Sure you did. You thought it was a potting-shed permit."

"You *distracted* me!"

The guests tittered.

Dad's grin went very wide, entertaining the guests the more while Aunt Fee's back went ramrod straight.

"Before we begin," my father said. "I have an O. Henry quote for my bride."

We all groaned. " 'There she plucked from my lapel the invisible strand of lint (the universal act of woman to proclaim ownership).' "

Aunt Fee nodded. "I'll rebut with George Meredith:

253

'The task of reclaiming a bad man is extremely seductive to good women.'"

Oh, my stars and garters, they were a perfect match.

The minister began the formal part of the ceremony, after which he asked if they had their own words to speak. They winged it perfectly. Not a dry eye in the house.

The scent of chocolate was to die for.

There was no meal at this late hour, but a lovely dessert buffet, so people thought the aroma of chocolate came from there.

Fiona and I knew better. We cried as we embraced. "Did you know?" she asked.

"Not until I saw your flower girl. He pulled one over on the best of us. I had no idea he'd planned an entire wedding!" I leaned in to whisper, "I didn't know and I'm a psychic sleuth, for heaven's sakes."

My father stuck his head between us. "That's why we didn't let you hem Kelsey's dress," he whispered.

Ack! "How much do you know . . . about what I might or might not . . . know?" I dared ask.

"You remind me of your mother . . . more every day."

Neither Fiona nor I asked for clarification. We took him at face value.

The newlyweds stayed for less than an hour, until a white limo whisked them off to the airport and a trip to the South Seas, which is all my father would say, besides, "I'll call you and I love you," as he waved.

People walked them to the limo and left. I watched Tunney tuck Dolly into his car from the upper window. The band had another half hour to play, so Werner asked them to continue.

I couldn't believe my eyes, but I turned and saw my

mother in the next window looking down, watching the limo carrying Dad and Fee roll from my parking lot.

"Mom," I whispered in my mind, and she turned to me, her eyes glistening.

"You're happy for them, aren't you?"

She fisted her hand against her heart and nodded.

"But you miss them."

Another nod as she started to fade, and my last sight was of her blowing me a kiss.

Werner walked up to me. "Why so sad?"

"My mom," I said. "It's natural—"

"You look like you might have seen her. Did you?"

"For the second time in twenty years. The first was at Sherry's wedding."

The band played a slow waltz. Werner and I danced, as did Robin and Glen, Eve and Jay, who we talked into staying. The lights dimmed, compliments of Dante.

Werner kissed me as we waltzed, so romantic, so slow, just us, until . . .

My eyes overflowed, dripped slowly down my face, as I realized what I saw before me.

"No reason to be sad, Cupcake," Dolly said, young as the day she and Dante had met, dancing in his arms like they'd never been apart.

I knew only one thing for sure: She'd died in her Katharine Hepburn dress, the one like the wedding gown from *The Philadelphia Story*. Two unions had been ordained this night, and only I knew it.

"Why cry?" Dolly asked, eliciting Dante's killer grin, and her eyes twinkled. "We're spending eternity together, here, Mad, with you."

Vintage Magic Purses

The first purse you saw in the story was Dolly's bright orange square handbag. Definitely plastic, probably from a five-and-dime store, circa the nineteen sixties. The name is molded inside: "Jaclyn-ette." It's about twelve inches square with an accordion fold, it can get up to about five inches wide. It has a mail pouch on the front with a brass latch and grommets, and brass rings that connect the handles. They're not adjustable. Inside are two zip compartments, one on each side, and the center is a zip compartment of its own. All zippers are metal.

The second bag is a beaded white clutch with a snap closure, about six inches wide and three and a half deep. The corded interior has "Corde Bead" stamped in gold with other lettering that I can't read inside.

The black-and-white beaded bag, top gold circle-over-ball

snap closure, same size, has "Grandee" stamped on the satin interior.

The fourth is a gold-spun weave with rhinestones sprinkled throughout. Very flat. About seven inches wide, three inches deep. One back pocket. It has a flap the full size of the purse with a snap at the bottom front. Stamped inside the cream satin interior is "Magid" with a pair of wings beneath the word.

I adore the black satin bag. Wider at the bottom at about nine curved inches to six straight at the top, it flares inside its frame and has a bow at the top center. The cream satin interior has a cursive "L" printed and a cursive "PM" above a circle. In the circle, I can only make out the word "Rochette." This is the only brand of the set that I could not verify. And there's more writing that I can't make out. If you know this brand I'd love to hear from you.

You can see pictures of the bags on my website at www.annetteblair.com/vintage_magic_handbags.htm.

I found all the bags above at Cressie's Vintage Boutique in Goshen, Indiana, 1100 North Chicago Avenue, at the Old Bag Factory, second floor.

Special thanks to Crescencia for a lovely visit.

www.cressiesvintageboutique.vpweb.com

And Then You Dye

A Needlecraft Mystery

Betsy is a natural-born yarnsmith—so it's only fitting that some of her favorite items to stock come from the dye-works of Hailey Brent. Hailey makes hand-dyed knitting wool, silk, soy, and corn yarns. She uses only natural vegetable dyes, creating soft and beautiful colors. Which means her yarns are expensive, but well worth it.

Unfortunately, someone thinks they're worth killing for.

When Hailey's body is discovered shot dead in her workshop, Betsy must wring the truth from a bevy of colorful suspects. Because the truth just might mean the difference between living—and dyeing...

Praise for the Needlecraft Mysteries

"Ferris's fans will be charmed." —*Publishers Weekly*

"Ferris's characterizations are top-notch, and the action moves along at a crisp pace." —*Booklist*

"A comfortable fit for mystery readers who want to spend an enjoyable time with interesting characters."
—*St. Paul Pioneer Press*

Free Counted Cross-Stitch Pattern Included!

Springtime in Fort Connor, Colorado, is a breeze until a veteran con man shows up in town. Everyone— including the House of Lambspun knitters—is up in arms, and once again it's up to Kelly Flynn to untangle the threads of a complicated crime…

FROM NATIONAL BESTSELLING AUTHOR
MAGGIE SEFTON

Close Knit Killer
A Knitting Mystery

Kelly's good friend, the owner of the House of Lambspun, is looking to turn an old storage building into a classroom space for her shop's spinners and weavers. But when a familiar face is found dead in his car outside of Lambspun, Kelly and her friends will need to focus on sorting through a long list of fleeced suspects to catch the killer…

DELICIOUS RECIPES AND KNITTING PATTERN INCLUDED!

maggiesefton.com
facebook.com/maggieseftonauthor
facebook.com/TheCrimeSceneBooks
penguin.com